Southern Dreams

DIARY OF OLIVIA BELLAMEAD

BOOKS BY DIANN SHADDOX

A Faded Cottage

Whispering Fog

Miranda

Spirits of Sacred Mountain

The Gatekeeper I

Hidden Dreams

Diary of Olivia Bellamead

Diann Shaddox

Diary of Olivia Bellamead

By Diann Shaddox

ISBN: 978-1-7371331-2-4
ISBN: 978-1-7371331-3-1
ISBN: 978-1-7371331-4-8

Eagle Quill Publishing
www.eaglequillpublishing.com
First print Edition May 2022
Printed in the United States of American
Diary of Olivia Bellamead Copyright © 2014, Diann Shaddox

Acknowledgment

To Marsha Tolleson Rhodes, my editor:

Thank you for your encouragement, kindness, your patience, and the many hours you have spent working with me. I will be forever grateful for everything you've done.

Hidden Dreams Cover Art:

Crossways, circa 1815, Aiken, SC. Crossways originally served as the main home for an antebellum plantation. Crossways is rich in history, style, and symmetry with generously proportioned rooms and restored architectural details. Over 200 years old now, Crossways represents the grace, ease, and elegance of a time past.

The Diary of Olivia Bellamead

Prelude

Her body shook hearing the gunfire in the side yard. Her heart was pounding, but not from the deafening noise of the rifles, but the young man behind her peering out her father's office window. He wasn't very tall, but his facial features were strong with high cheekbones and she could feel the affectionate stare. She knew a lady shouldn't look back at him, but…never doing as she was told, she looked. The young man smiled down on her with the bluest eyes causing a tingle to flow through her body. Alas, after that Fourth of July picnic, the man left the next day riding north to his home. He left knowing many men at the picnic weren't pleased that a Northerner had joined in the festivities, since the tales of war were stirring.

This particular Fourth of July picnic, Olivia Rose Bellamead, a young Southern belle, arranged engagement to Jackson Seth Montgomery was to be announced by her parents. However, Olivia made it a priority to meet the dashing Yankee at the celebration, named Andrew Robert Drake who changed the course of both of their lives.

•••

Chapter One

"July 4th, 1861"

The crispness of the morning was warmed by the sun radiating through the light layer of fog, which was lying over the valleys surrounding Bella Oak Plantation, the home of William Randell Bellamead and his family since 1844. This July fourth, 1861, was to be the most extraordinary picnic for Bella Oak Plantation and the people of South Carolina. This was not a celebration for the Union anymore, but for the New South that was rising up taking on their own political agenda, with a new president, Jefferson Davis. South Carolina had seceded from the Union the winter before. The Southerners stood tall with assurance that all would be well. Everyone would attend this event, including the governor and especially Olivia Bellamead's fiancé, Jackson Seth Montgomery, the eldest son of Zachariah Rory Montgomery who lived on the Montgomery Plantation adjacent to Bella Oak. That early morning the grand plantation of Bella Oak was buzzing with excitement as everyone woke to a gorgeous day.

"Olivia, quit playing possum I know you're awake."

"Annie… you close those drapes," Olivia growled pulling the quilt over her head.

Annie said softly quivering with excitement, "I'm watching everyone run around like bees flying to their hive as they get prepared for this picnic,"

The long drapes became the young girl's shield as she leaned over against the open window peering out into the massive yard.

"Oh…" Annie bragged, "Bella Oak is coming alive, and I think the plantation knows everyone is going to be here soon. Somehow the grass looks greener and the oaks look taller! Even the moss is fluffier! This is going to be our plantation's day to shine. Bella Oak is becoming a true Southern belle."

"Oh, please, Annie," moaned the exasperated girl, sliding her head back under the quilts. "You're talking silly; a plantation can't be a Southern belle. Now…close the drapes!"

"Yes it can. You better get up. Sadie was here earlier and you didn't even move," Annie announced as the breeze blew her long, light blonde hair over her face. "You need to get out of that bed, and we should go downstairs now."

"No," Olivia whimpered plopping her dark brown curls back on her pillow. "I'm plum tuckered out," she whispered, swishing her hair with her hand and realizing that she had forgotten to wear her nightcap to bed.

"Well, if you hadn't stayed up so late sitting outside on the verandah with Jackson Montgomery, you wouldn't be so tired," Annie declared.

"Oh, Annie, the light's too bright with the drapes open so wide. Please," Olivia begged pulling the flower-patterned quilt tighter up over her face.

"The men are setting up the bandstand," Annie announced. "We better get ready."

"Annie, close those drapes. They might see you in your nightgown!" Olivia demanded peeking out from under the quilt with her green eyes squinting in the bright sunlight.

"What did you talk about with Jackson last night?" questioned Annie. "He did stay until very late?"

"Annie, what do you mean what did I talk about last night? Were you spying on me?"

"Sure," the young girl giggled. "He sho' does carry on about his plantation. I fell asleep sitting here on the window seat listening to you, but I did wake up in time..."

"Annie Bellamead… what do you mean in time?"

"To see that nasty kiss. You sho' didn't look happy," Annie added giggling. "He rattles on a lot about nothing."

"Annie, I can't believe you were spying on me and yes that kiss was awful. You're finally making some sense. He is as boring as having a conversation with that old tom cat out back. He's full of foolish gibberish."

"Maybe you can change him after you're married…ooh," Annie shivered again.

"What?"

"I'm glad it's you and not me marrying him," Annie laughed, "Now, you better get up."

"Annie Bellamead, are you saying something bad about someone? Lordy, everyone will be turning over in their graves wondering what happened to sweet Annie!" Olivia proclaimed.

"Olivia, hush!"

"Girls!"

"I told you," Annie chuckled. "You're in trouble now. The men have finished the bandstand and the musicians are tuning their instruments. We should hurry."

"Olivia Rose," came a call from the door, "you climb out of that bed this instant." The long, flowing brownish dress rustled as the beautiful woman walked into the bedroom. The woman looked so young with her light hair pulled up with ringlets hanging down around her smooth pale face. She quickly moved over by Olivia's bed folding her hands together with so much composure.

"Mother, I'm tired." Olivia grumbled, rolling over hiding in the feather bed. "Mama Beulah sent Sadie up here over an hour ago to get you girls up."

"I was up, Mother," Annie answered, leaning her head back against the wall taking in a deep breath of the pungent smell of smoked barbeque flowing in the open window. Ruth smiled over at her younger daughter. Then, she turned around. The woman's shoulders tightened with her eyes staring back at her older daughter Olivia.

"Well, this time next year, young lady, you will be the wife of a plantation owner and there sho' won't be time to lie around in bed all morning."

"Mother, I still have a few months of freedom," Olivia muttered from under the quilt. Ruth's dress swished in the quiet room moving near Olivia. Her tiny, pure white hand pulled the quilts down uncovering the stunning girl.

"Now, honey," she said in a soft voice as she smoothed back the brown curls and looked into those green eyes, "Jackson isn't that bad. He is, at least, handsome and he will be here soon."

"Dagnabbit, being the wife of a plantation owner doesn't sound fun," Olivia whispered not wanting her mother to hear, but those blue eyes looked back with a warning that a Southern lady would never use words like that.

"Annie…sweetie," Ruth asked walking over to her daughter who was still sitting next to the window. She leaned in giving her a hug, using her fingers, gently combing back Annie's soft hair from her face. "Have you seen your brothers?"

"No ma'am, it's been quiet."

"Olivia Rose!" Ruth said in a stern voice twirling around peering back at her older daughter who wasn't moving, still hiding under the pile of quilts.

"Yes, ma'am," Olivia responded sitting up in bed, using her hands to comb the tousled hair sticking out.

"I declare, you and Benjamin sho' took after your father," Ruth muttered leaving the room.

"Alright… Let's go downstairs…Annie, stop that grinning," Olivia moaned, standing from the bed stretching her arms out wide. The two girls made their way down the long staircase and sat at the dining room table covered with its lace tablecloth that had come all the way from England, a gift for their mother from Sir James Bellamead their grandfather. The crystal goblets in the huge hutch on the back wall were sparkling along with Ruth's silver a backdrop behind them with more silver trays on the sideboard shining brightly. A large, dark woman with a frown on her round face came into the room. Olivia swallowed. Her body stiffened. Olivia, always getting her way, smiled up at the squinty brown eyes peering down on her. The plump older woman's head shook back and forth,

"I swanny, Miss Olivia," her lips pursed together, "I don't know what I'm going to do with you, child." The woman set a plate of grits and eggs in front of the girls.

"Mama Bea, I was tired this morning," Olivia insisted, "We have plenty of time before the picnic."

Olivia knew that she was always riling up the old woman, but a hint of smile was coming on Mama Bea's dark face as her chubby cheeks puffed up.

"Child, yo' needs to eat," she snapped, "and yo' don't has that much time," she answered shaking her head as she shuffled out of the room.

Annie opened her mouth to reply but was hushed by a look from Olivia.

"Annie," Olivia gave her sister a stare with her green eyes meeting her younger sister's blue eyes, "now, don't you say anything about last night."

"What in tarnation is that ruckus," Ruth called out from the back of the house. Olivia smiled when she heard the front door open and then slam shut. She was saved at least for a little while. "Benjamin Randell Bellamead," Ruth called back, "you get upstairs and clean up."

Benjamin, Olivia's younger brother had the same green eyes that she had. He peered around the door of the dining room and stared over at his sisters who were still sitting at the dining room table. He grinned. Dust covered him from his head to his snakeskin leather boots.

"You're just now eating breakfast?" the young boy questioned.

"Father is on his way to his office. You'd better get done," Annie said in her soft voice.

"Where have you been?" Olivia whispered as she stood from the table and moved near the doorway.

"Yesterday, I found a rabbit hole, one out in the east pasture. This morning," he answered excitedly trying to stand taller than he was, "I went and shot me some rabbits."

"You took Joseph, I presume."

"Yep," Benjamin answered as he kept looking back at Olivia. It was like looking into a mirror they were so alike and it wasn't only in looks.

"Benjamin, you better get cleaned up, if Father's on his way," she whispered.

When the two heard the door open from the back of the room, Benjamin swiftly turned to leave racing from the room and Olivia rushed to her chair. Mama Bea walked into the room missing Benjamin by only a few seconds.

"Miss Annie, youse eats like a bird, and Miss Olivia," she shook her head, "youse eats like an old hound dog. Youse needs to slo' down, or youse won't fit in yo' mother's wedding dress next spring."

Strawberry Jam oozed out of the warm biscuit dripping down from Olivia's hand onto her plate.

"Mama Bea, I couldn't eat much last night around Jackson. He's worse than you watching me eat." She puckered her face, "I'm hungry," she added with her mouth full, swallowing with big gulps.

"Sadie, youse come and cleans this room up," Mama Bea bellowed toward the kitchen. "Now child, let's get yo' dress. Mister Jackson will be here soon asking fur you."

Those dark brown eyes of Mama Bea followed Olivia's every move. She watched the young girl slide her chair gracefully back under the table. Olivia lifted her nightgown up off the floor. She wiggled her bare toes on the cool, smooth oak wood floors and stepped one measured step at a time slowly going up the magnificent, wooden staircase. The mahogany front door opened wide. Olivia's father stepped into the foyer. Olivia stopped on the stairs still holding onto her long nightgown looking down on her father.

"Olivia Rose," William stood with his green eyes peering up at her.

"Yes, Father," she softly called down to him.

"You're not worrying your mother this early in the morning, are you?" he asked, seeing she wasn't dressed yet.

"No Sir," she assured with Mama Bea's eyes still observing her as she peered down at her from the top of the stairs. William turned his head from her hiding his smile as he opened his office door. He knew she was so like him, not caring about following rules. His being a lawyer was ironic. A loud bump came from Benjamin and Joseph's bedroom upstairs.

"Now, Master Benjamin, youse stop that wrestling," Mama Bea called out hurrying down the long hallway quickly going into the boy's bedroom.

Olivia swung open her bedroom door. Lying on the bed was a beautiful, light cream dress with raspberry colored swirls woven throughout, so delicate and beautiful. Her mother had brought the magnificent dress in Charleston just for this summer's picnic. Olivia would be the true Southern belle for this picnic and the news of her upcoming wedding next year would be announced this morning.

"Lordy Mercy, Miss Olivia, youse not undressed yet," Mama Bea declared coming into the bedroom swishing her large dress as she moved to the bed. "Take those sleeping clothes off, child, youse daydreaming again, aren't ya."

Mama Bea swiftly reached over with her large hands busily lifting Olivia's nightgown off. Olivia finished layering all of her undergarments. Annie who was already dressed sat on her bed watching her sister. Mama Bea's fluffed the magnificent dress in the air. Annie sighed as Olivia stepped into the dress and then twirled in circles letting the gorgeous dress flow gracefully showing its bright red raspberry color.

"Oh...Olivia, you're so beautiful," Annie announced with her eyes so enamored, studying her sister who was four years older. Olivia had the round face of her father with the small nose and smile that curved into her cheeks so perfectly with those dark green eyes that could see into the soul. She was a true Bellamead, just like Benjamin, with perseverance and stubbornness always enduring, not letting anything or anyone get in her way.

"Miss Olivia's the prettiest girl around these parts, and yo' is the prettiest youngin." Mama Bea smiled with her cheeks puffing up looking at both young girls. Mama Bea had taken care of Olivia and her siblings since they were born. She treated them like they were her own children. She had worked for Aunt Violia Walden in

Charleston but had joined the Bellamead family after Olivia was born. She soon became a part of the family. Olivia sat down on the stool in front of the mahogany dresser and the old woman picked up the pearl-handled brush, a gift William had brought from England for his daughters.

"Youse furgot yo'r night cap again," Mama Bea scorned, trying to untangle Olivia's long silken hair. She cupped the hair gently in her large hands making the long brown hair fall down in its perfect curls.

"Olivia!" called out Benjamin loudly tapping at the bedroom door.

"Benjamin, what do you want?"

"Are you decent?"

"Yes, come on in and quit yelling before Mother hears you."

"Don't squirm so much," Mama Bea scolded trying to hold onto Olivia's hair.

"Sorry, Mama Bea," Olivia said quickly turning her head forward so the curls fell precisely on her bare shoulders.

"Sit still, let me get yo' hair done," Mama Bea snapped. The door flew open with Benjamin stepping into the room with Joseph following close behind. Mama Bea moaned when she saw that Benjamin wasn't properly dressed. He rushed to the window pulling back the drapes.

"What are you up to?" questioned Olivia curiously. She stood from the stool, pulling her hair away from Mama Bea.

"Father was downstairs working in his office when a strange man, not much older than we are, rode up on his dark horse. Father hurried out onto the verandah to meet him. I could hear them talking. The man is not from around here; he talked differently, with an accent. They were discussing the Union versus the Confederates."

"What does he want?" questioned Olivia looking at her brother who was always so jubilant and excited by anything out of the ordinary.

Benjamin held back the drapes, "I don't know," he whispered, peering out the bedroom window. "They are outside on the verandah. You need to come over here and see," he added waving his arm at her. "Look at father and the young man… They're so intense."

Olivia's petticoat layered dress swished as she walked in the quiet room to the window. Mama Bea frowned with the hairbrush swinging in the air.

"Miss Olivia, youse gets away from that window, yo' father…sho' is going to be upset at yo' spying on him. Tain't fittin'. Come over here and act like a lady," Mama Bea admonished as she twisted her head back and forth, knowing she couldn't stop those two when they set their mind to something.

Mama Bea's squinted eyes looked over at the younger Bellamead children, Mary Ann *Annie* Bellamead and Joseph David Bellamead, age twelve, twins. They had Ruth's demeanor, blue eyes, and light hair. They sat so quietly always doing what they were told, so different from the two older Bellamead children.

A huge grin covered Benjamin's face, "He's something, isn't he?"

"Yes," Olivia's voice wavered in a soft whisper, but her eyes didn't move away from the young man with brawny facial features who was standing next to her father.

The man wasn't real tall, but taller than her father. He had wavy, light brown hair. He was dressed in black riding boots, camel trousers, a burgundy tailcoat, white shirt, and black vest. He was so handsome, mesmerizing her.

"I heard he's from Philadelphia. Jonas said he is…a Yankee," whispered Benjamin breathlessly. "He knows what is going on with the war up North."

Neither Benjamin nor Olivia would move from the window, both awestruck. Their eyes stayed glued peering down on the verandah. Silently, they listened to the two men who were now deep in conversation.

"William, this isn't good. My father is worried about you because he heard that Scott is advancing on the South," the young man began; his words were strong and precise. "He believes you should take your family and sail back to England where they'll be safe."

"Andrew, your father is a kind man. I have heard the news, but I'm not leaving Bella Oak. This is my home and I have a plantation to run," William assured. "I'm very grateful for John to send you here to warn me, but our Confederate Army is growing and we will be fine. It's just a matter of the Union recognizing us as a new country. It shouldn't take long."

Olivia's mind was spinning thinking to herself. His name is Andrew. She began to say it over and over in her mind.

"I'm not so sure," Andrew answered anxiously with his head shaking back and forth.

"Son, we just had more states that seceded this spring and they have made Richmond our new capital."

"I understand," Andrew agreed tightening his shoulders, "but there are four other states that are staying with the Union. The South is not organized or trained enough to take on the US Army. This isn't going to end well for either side, but especially the South."

"I talked to the governor, just the other day and he has assurance that things will be over soon, William added convincingly.

"Father is very worried and believes you need to leave," Andrew protested rubbing his hands together.

"Son, the South is stronger than you think. I have learned a lot living here for the past twenty years."

"Yes," Andrew answered, "I understand." His lips turned into a smile, "Father told me you would be stubborn. Sir, I'm here to help your family and I will do whatever you want me to do."

"The Confederacy is growing each day," William spoke in his strong authoritative voice. "Don't look so worried, son. This war will end soon and all will be better than before," he answered patting Andrew on the back. His words were confident, as if he was in a courtroom defending the Confederacy from the Union on his own.

"This talk is troubling me." Andrew answered with his eyebrows squeezed together frowning. "Sir," he continued shaking his head peering down at the verandah floor. "I have seen the Union Army, and President Lincoln isn't backing down. Look at all the revenue and taxes that the Union is losing. The Union will not back down. Please," he pleaded, "you must get ready."

"Son, you worry something awful for such a young man."

"William," Andrew paused taking in a deep breath. "On my travels here I stayed the night not far from where a battle was fought June tenth, at Great Bethel, Virginia, not good."

"I heard about that battle from some men in Charleston, but, we, the Confederacy, won. The Union Army wasn't prepared for that battle and our army only lost one man."

"Yes," Andrew sighed, "but, Sir," with his body tensing again, "the Union is getting better equipped and my father found out that President Lincoln is calling for more men, hundreds of thousands of men for the Union Army. These battles are escalating and you need to prepare."

"Fair enough, I have been warned," a smile came on William's face. "Come on, son, let's have a drink. You are staying for the picnic, aren't you? You also look tired and can leave tomorrow after you rest." William turned, opened the wooden front door, and walked into the foyer. "We will talk more tonight after the picnic."

Benjamin moved back from the window letting the drapes fall back down. "Dang it, that's not good, if the North is preparing so much."

"I wonder who Andrew is?" Olivia asked scrunching her nose, not paying any attention to her brother.

Benjamin shook his head that he didn't know…. "Andrew sho' is worried."

"He and his father must be good friends of father's to risk his life riding down from the North to warn us," Olivia surmised, tightly puckering her lips.

"I already told Father I was ready to fight, but he won't let me join the Confederate Army, not yet." Benjamin continued talking, staring off not listening to his sister.

"Lordy Mercy, youse don't need to worry yo' mother so with this kind of talk." Mama Bea scowled staring at the young boy. She nervously began picking up clothes around the room and straightening up everything.

"But…Mama Bea, I'm fourteen, I'm old enough to go fight and show those Yankees a thing or two," he protested. "I can out shoot many of the men around these parts."

Mama Bea shook her head, "Youse needs to get dressed! That's what youse needs to do! Everyone will be here soon," she answered turning back around muttering, "Yo' two young'uns, I declare! Stop a'talkin' about war. This is spossed to be a happy day."

"I'm aiming to go this fall and become a Rebel soldier. You just wait and see," Benjamin declared.

"Lordy mercy, that child, gwanna wear me out," Mama Bea insisted, looking back at Olivia.

She turned to Benjamin, "Now, stop yo' piddlin' and get yo' nice clothes on."

Benjamin raced out of the bedroom, as always with Joseph following him. He knew he had to dress befitting the eldest son of a wealthy plantation owner. He stopped outside of the bedroom door, turning around with his head peering back into Olivia's room.

"Olivia, you do look lovely," he called back to his sister, who was still standing holding the drapes staring out the window.

"Thank you," she said, letting the drapes fall from her soft white hands. She turned from the window looking back at her brother.

Smoothing down her stunning flowing dress, she straightened her shoulders and held up her head impatiently sashaying to the bedroom door.

"I'm going downstairs and see if Mother can use some help with anything," Olivia announced.

Mama Bea looked over questioning her, "Now child, yo' ain't going to bother yo' father or that young man? I see mischief in yo' face."

"Mama Bea, I'm engaged to Jackson. I will be good, but I do need to welcome all of our visitors," she snapped back.

"Uh hum," Mama Bea moaned as she kept tidying up the bedroom staring at the young beautiful girl who could outfox a fox.

Olivia was on a mission; she had to meet Andrew. His voice and the way he stood had drawn her in. She had never felt emotions stirring like she felt now. She gently lifted her flowing dress in her hands scurrying down the long curving staircase, not as lady-like as she should since she didn't have any watchful eyes on her. The foyer was quiet except for her shoes tapping onto the wood floor. The tapping became rhythmic as she moved near her father's office.

However, she was intercepted by her mother who was glowing with pride, "Olivia, good, you can help me check over my list to be shor everything's done," she added grabbing hold of her daughter. "Honey, you are gorgeous! You are a true Southern belle if I ever saw one. I can't wait until your father and Jackson see you."

Olivia was more interested in the young man in her father's office seeing her than Jackson, but wasn't going to tell her mother. Their shoes in unison began to tap on the wooden floor. The voices from the office became clearer. Olivia slowed down her pace, turned around, and peered inside the door, but her mother continued on pulling her to the back of the home. The women stepped outside into the bright sun.

They could see a composed chaos over the grounds of Bella Oak. The plantation was alive with voices and people hurrying about. The sun was shining down on the plantation and the smell of freshly baked pies along with the hickory smoked barbeque blended in the air with the gardenia bush's sweet blooms surrounding the porch of the massive home.

The women strolled to the side of the home where the tables were set perfectly under a group of old live oaks with their huge limbs covered in Spanish moss, gently fanning the tables from a light breeze. The bandstand was ready. The musicians were dressed in their crisp uniforms setting up their instruments preparing to stay the entire day. Ruth's body was quivering with excitement. This was her day, her picnic, and her family along with their glorious plantation.

"The day is going to be wonderful," Ruth announced as she clasped her tiny, smooth hands together, so thrilled with her enthusiasm growing.

Olivia smiled at her mother knowing that when the music started, her mother's social graces would take over as the lady of Bella Oak and she would stand poised and ready. Olivia paused for a moment to assess the elegant decorations and thought to herself that her sister had been correct earlier that morning; Bella Oak was a Southern Bell.

The black wrought iron gates with the name Bella Oak were opened wide. Their tall brick columns on each side covered in wisteria and ivy were welcoming everyone to the magnificent plantation. Dust was flying behind buggies wheeling down the oak tree-lined path that led the way to the plantation home. A few young boys were seeing to all of the horses and buggies with Jonas watching their every move. Jonas stood dressed in his finest clothes with his smile brimming from ear to ear. All the men of the county nodded their heads to say thank you to the old man who had seen to the buggies since 1844. Olivia could hear people talking, laughing, and children squealing as each family found their perfect spot to throw down quilts in the soft green grass to enjoy the picnic.

"We better get inside. Your father will be ready and we mustn't keep him waiting." Ruth put her hand on her daughter's arm as she turned walking to the back of the home.

The small woman hurried up the steps and took in a deep breath to get her composure back, ready for the picnic to begin. The plantation home was becoming quiet inside with everyone busy out in the enormous yard. The two women slowly walked to the foyer. William was waiting in the foyer by the front door with Benjamin, Joseph, and Annie standing by his side. He stood straight and tall, so charismatic and handsome with tiny streaks of gray wisping throughout his dark, thick hair. When he saw Ruth and Olivia walking toward him, a smile was emerged causing his dimples to stand out.

"My dears, I am a proud man right now." He bent down kissing Ruth wrapping his arms around his tiny wife. "My dear Ruth, Bella Oak is ready. Let's go begin this picnic."

Ruth bobbed her head and looked up into the eyes of her husband with a smile illuminating her flawless creamy face. William's pride showed with Ruth next to him walking to the front door. James, dressed in his finest blue jacket and blue britches, opened the door wide. The proud Bellamead family stepped out onto the verandah seeing the vast crowd of people who were speckling the grounds.

Benjamin took Olivia's arm and they stood beside William, while Annie and Joseph stood beside Ruth, a picture-perfect family. The warmth of the sun was radiating down on the grand plantation and there was freshness in the morning air. The flowers were blooming as if on demand and the tall pines were standing guard in the gentle breeze. Olivia's eyes peered out over the host of people from the area. Many had ridden all the way from Charleston and Colombia and stayed nearby on some of the other plantations just to be at this picnic.

This year the faces of the men were drawn and Olivia knew the war was bothering them along with her father, but nothing was going to interfere with these festivities. She did notice that Andrew wasn't anywhere out in the crowd. She could feel a stare from the window of her father's office and looked around to see that Andrew had stayed inside.

There, down at the bottom of the steps of the verandah was Jackson Montgomery standing by his father Zachariah Montgomery. He stood tall, dressed in his maroon coat, dark britches, and perfectly shined boots. He smiled at Olivia as he stepped upon the verandah. Her mother gave her a look and Olivia smiled up at Jackson as he stationed himself on her other side. It was plain to everyone that Olivia had two escorts, her brother and Jackson.

Olivia knew next spring the Montgomerys and Bellameads would soon combine the two most prosperous plantations in the South blending two affluent bloodlines. Olivia's father, William, had graduated from Cambridge to become a man of nobility in Charleston in 1839 along with his new wife, Edith Elizabeth. They settled into life in Charleston with their first child to be born that fall. Arthur Morris was dividing up farm land that lay along a huge river not far from Charleston. The land was just right for cotton and rice. When one of the men backed out of the deal leaving over fourteen hundred acres, William and Zachariah Montgomery stepped in. William took eight hundred acres leaving six hundred for Zachariah. They each began building their massive homes with William hiring Cyrus as foreman to see to his plantation.

That fall Edith Elizabeth gave birth to a son, but William's happiness was short lived when both mother and child died, devastating him. With sorrow in his heart, he continued on building his plantation home, but put Cyrus in charge to finish it.

Then, one Christmas a few years later changed William's life. He was invited to Charleston to a home of a friend. There he met a young girl of seventeen from the Charleston society, Ruth Ann Walden. She had the bluest eyes and light golden hair lying in beautiful long ringlets surrounding her oval face. He couldn't take his eyes off her at the Christmas Ball. They were married that next spring when she turned eighteen in the year of 1844 and she was delighted to move to their new home that they named Bella Oak Plantation.

Chapter Two

"Blue Eyes Watching"

Governor Pickens, a short stocky man, made his way through the crowd carefully stepping up onto the verandah. William met him with a handshake. The two men's worried eyes showed their apprehension. Both men stood enthralled watching the new Confederate flag of the Confederate States of America, the *Stars and Bars*, a flag with seven stars in the blue field and wide stripes set in place. William turned back to the crowd of people all watching with trepidation. He held his hands into the air with everyone becoming quiet.

"Welcome to Bella Oak Plantation, my wonderful home. This is now a celebration for the New South," everybody cheered, "the Confederacy!"

Silence fell over the crowd of people as he pulled his arms down to his side.

"Before I introduce our special guest, I do have one announcement. I would like to add," he said taking a breath, "next spring, my lovely daughter Olivia Bellamead is to wed Jackson Montgomery right here on Bella Oak and everyone is invited to the wedding."

The crowd cheered and applauded. Jackson's body puffed out like a pleased rooster. He slipped his arm around Olivia and they stepped forward next to William. Their attention turned from William to the couple, and then Jackson led Olivia back to the family. Benjamin looked over at his sister. He shook his head slowly with empathy in his eyes understanding the sorrow in Olivia's eyes. However, it was now official; she was to wed Jackson next spring.

William continued talking. "This is a glorious day and a perfect day to rejoice and enjoy the fruits of all of our hard work, but first...." He turned to his side, leaning over patting his hand compassionately on the Governor's back, "I would like to introduce you to the first Governor of the independent State of South Carolina, Governor Pickens."

Cheers screamed to the heavens and the small band began to play with excitement building. The Governor stepped forward with his shoulders squared, his face was worn and tired, but he smiled with his deep, powerful voice resonating across the grounds of Bella Oak.

"My dear South Carolinians, the news has spread and is true; the dignitaries assembled one cold winter day, adopting a new constitution, and dissolving our ties with the Union. We, the state of South Carolina became the first of many states to secede from the Union. I am proud to stand before you as part of the Confederate States of America."

Everyone applauded giving a standing ovation with screams and whistles echoing out into the fields.

"We tried unsuccessfully to find a peaceful resolution for the Union to relinquish Fort Sumter. We could not back down and a battle was fought without the loss of life," he grinned. "I might add. The Union garrison surrendered the fort, but there was a mishap and one man was killed and a few injured after the surrender. We allowed the Union soldiers to leave peacefully, but as all skirmishes, this didn't end well and was considered the initiation of war. As of April twelfth, we are at war with the Union and President Abraham Lincoln, to fight once more for our freedom and the right to live as we choose."

Shouts of enthusiasm screamed out from the crowd with loud cheers echoing.

"My South Carolinians," he swung his short arms in the air with perspiration growing on his brow, "our Confederate Army is prepared for battle under our new leader, President of the Confederates States of America, Jefferson Davis," he stopped talking his arms fell down by his side and the crowd became deathly silent. "God bless us and our troops and may Al-l-l-mighty God show mercy on us."

A sigh of relief came over his strained face stepping back. His arms once more spread out wide, turning his tired eyes to William, "Now it's time to enjoy this marvelous plantation. Let the festivities began."

He raised his arms high in the air, the band began to play, and everyone cried out as one and all began to sing, *I wish I was in the land of cotton, Old times there are not forgotten; Look away! Look away! Look away, Dixie's Land!"* the song echoed out over the land with pride taking the place of worry on many of the men's faces.

The South would rise up and become victorious. Benjamin's body squirmed as he sang along with everyone. He kept ringing his hands in a washing movement not able to stand still. His strong voice with the perfect tempo was overtaking the other family members. When the song was ending, Olivia anxiously clasped her hands together in front of her. She slowly turned her head, peering behind herself. She became spellbound and didn't move. Andrew was staring at her from her father's office window. She swiftly turned her head back around trying to be discreet but could feel the warmth growing on her face as she blushed.

The men in Confederate grey army uniforms standing out to the side of the large home raised their riffles and began to fire making Olivia shiver. But, was it because of the deafening blasts or Andrew?

She couldn't resist and turned once more with her eyes meeting those blue eyes. A tingling sensation washed over her entire body. Andrew smiled down on her with such newness and her lips curled into a smile knowing she wasn't acting like a lady who was now officially engaged. Benjamin grabbed hold of her before Jackson noticed. He gave her a stern look as if to say, *Discretion, dear sister. Discretion*! However, a grin emerged on his face.

The guns became silent and the family stepped off of the verandah greeting the crowd. Olivia didn't get a chance to peer back up to the window. The well-wishers grabbed hold of her turning her body to face them. Miss Libby and her group of gossips (the small town's new women's society for the county) were the first reaching out to Olivia.

"My dear this is the greatest news and we will plan the most fabulous wedding this county has ever had," stated the short gray-haired woman with the neck of her dress pulled tightly up to her chin. She turned quick letting her stubby fingers grab hold of Ruth. "We need to have everything in its correct social order," Miss Libby added.

"Yes, Miss Violia Walden will have to come and join us in the preparation," one of the women offered, so thrilled to be having Charleston society assisting them.

"I'm shor' Aunt Violia would be glad to stay a while with us and plan the wedding next spring as soon as the weather clears. She doesn't like to travel in bad weather," Ruth assured.

"This is what the town needs to plan, a marvelous wedding, not talk of the war. By next spring, the war will be over," Miss Libby said firmly, with Ruth and all the women nodding their heads yes in agreement. "My dear Ruth, we have a lot of work ahead, but this will be the best wedding for the county."

Olivia wasn't paying any attention to the busy bodies. Her head turned from the group of women looking out over the crowd. She spotted her father standing with a group of men away from the festivities. There to his side was Andrew. All of the men seemed to be deep in conversation.

To Andrew's side was Benjamin standing erect trying to look older. Andrew was so debonair and so distinguished. She had never been around anyone like him. Her infatuation was growing. She saw Jackson in the group of men gazing back at her. She smiled, silently amused knowing that he thought she was staring at him.

"It's time to eat!" Cyrus called out, ringing the huge iron bell hanging in the side yard. The Governor and William hurried over to Ruth. Everyone quickly began to find a place to sit at the long tables and others were settling down on their quilts in the vast yard.

Brother Thomas led the crowd in prayer, "Our al-mighty God, we ask for blessings on this wonderful food and we ask for blessings on the new Confederacy. Uphold its cause, protect its people, and bring its soldiers home soon. Amen."

Jackson promptly moved over to Olivia's side. She scanned the crowd, but didn't see Andrew anywhere. Jackson put his arm around her waist pulling her close leading her to a long table with her father and mother along with the Governor sitting at the end. A plate full of barbeque and fresh bread along with vegetables was place in front of her. She anxiously nibbled at the food thankful that Jackson wasn't paying any attention to how she was eating. He was too enthralled in conversation with the man sitting next to him.

Governor Pickens, a heavyset man with hair curling around his ears finished his meal and stood trying to smile. A sense of duty was weighing on his shoulders.

"I regret that I shall have to depart before the dance. I am saddened that I shall miss dancing with the beautiful women of the county," Pickens announced.

His bushy gray eyebrow wrinkled as he took in a deep breath clearing his throat. As he looked out over the crowd, he paused squeezing his lips together.

Then he continued, "I do have business to see to, but this magnificent picnic will continue."

He dipped his head with his hat in his hand waving and turning to leave. William and a few men all with stern faces walked with the Governor to his carriage.

Olivia stood from the table searching the group of people finally spotting Andrew over to the side of the home deep in conversation with Cyrus. He wasn't sitting with the notable men of the county. She did notice many of the men staring at him and whispering with their sideways glances. They weren't happy to have a Yankee sharing a meal with them. But, the Yankee was a guest of William Bellamead and they were guests at Bella Oak, not a battlefield, so all the men of civility could do was gossip.

Chapter Three

"Andrew Robert Drake"

Jackson held onto Olivia's arm as they strolled leisurely around the huge grounds greeting everyone like good hosts. They stood under one of the old oaks in the shade watching many children run across the majestic yard playing games, listening to the sounds of laughter engulfing the plantation, and relishing in this eloquent event. The day moved on and everyone was beginning to rest, preparing themselves for the fresh fried apple pies, homemade churned ice cream, and the dance that would come later in the evening, when the day would cool.

During the hot afternoon, several of the women joined Ruth in the parlor of the home and the young damsels met upstairs in Olivia's room to rest. Little ones snuggled on quilts out in the yard under the shade of old trees quickly falling asleep with a soft breeze blowing over them. The verandah was full of young married couples looking out onto the plantation with dreams of their own futures.

Andrew and Jackson joined William in his office along with many of the men from the area to have a glass of whisky and cigar without the watchful eyes of the women. Olivia slipped off her long dress and sat down on her bed. The vigilant eyes of Mama Bea were watching her every move.

"Oh, this is such a wonderful picnic," whispered Camille, Olivia's longtime friend, who was lying on a cot next to Olivia's bed.

"Yes, isn't it!" Olivia replied lying back on her pillow with her eyes looking up to the high ceiling thinking of Andrew with a hidden smile coming over her face.

"The women shor' are carryin' on about your engagement," Camille added in a low voice. She slowly rolled over onto her side facing Olivia. "I reckon your wedding is going to be bigger than this picnic."

"Well, not everyone is happy," Olivia said softly, looking over at Etta.

Etta's dark hazel eyes were on fire with envy as she sneered at the two girls. Etta, the banker's daughter, had grown up in town not far from Camille's home. Etta was so opposite of Olivia. Etta with her long legs tucked under her thin body and clinched jaw sat in a dark corner of the room alone, scrutinizing the two girls.

"Don't worry about her; she's just jealous of you and Jackson."

"I know," Olivia sighed, feeling sorry for Etta. She now understood caring for someone who was unattainable and how much Etta must care for Jackson. Olivia secretly wished that Etta had won Jackson's heart and that she was the one who was engaged to Jackson. Camille eyes were staring off.

"Camille, you're dreaming again," Olivia whispered, giggling. "I did see you talking to Jerrold earlier in the day."

"Yes," the girl with the long red hair grinned, rolling over peering back at Olivia, "I can't wait until the dance. He has promised me many dances," her body shuddered and her eyes closed as she blushed turning her freckled face a bright red.

"I don't think you will have to worry about missing any of the dances. I saw how he was watching you when you weren't looking."

"Did you see that young man talking to Cyrus?" Camille asked. "Everyone was gawking at him."

"Yes," Olivia whispered softly.

"Jerrold said he was a Yankee. He doesn't look like some kind of a monster. I thought Yankees were mean and cruel."

"Camille, not all Yankees are like that. He is a friend of Father's," Olivia leaned over near her longtime friend.

Camille's eyes squinted looking back at her. Her head slowly moved as she was thinking. "I wonder," she began, "why a Northerner would risk riding down here through the South with all the talk of war."

"I have no idea," Olivia sighed, "but I'm going to find out," she added confidently.

"You let me know when you get the answer. He...shor' is different. I ain't seen anything like him before."

Olivia slowly nodded her head *yes*, "I do have to say he is handsome and very intriguing."

"Olivia Bellamead, do you have an interest in that young man."

"I'm just curious about him. His name is Andrew," she added not able to hide a smile appearing on her face.

"Olivia," Camille whispered sleepily, "you're going to get yourself in a heap of trouble."

"Ain't it grand," Olivia softly added falling back onto her bed. "Are you going to spy on me while I get in trouble or are you going with me?" She looked over and Camille was sound asleep. She laughed.

Olivia just couldn't rest. Her mind continued seeing those blue eyes from earlier staring at her from the office window. She quietly climbed out of her bed stepping over some of the other girls lying on pallets on the multicolor wool rug. She sat down at the window seat, her soft velvety hands pulled back the drapes peering out onto the plantation.

Mama Bea's attentive eyes weren't letting her out of her sight knowing Olivia should be resting. Olivia could see the massive grounds were quiet and only a few people were walking around. Even the band members were resting under an old oak so they would be ready for the dance later in the afternoon.

Large grey clouds were building in the blue sky telling there would be a storm that evening; at least the cloud cover would cool things down. Voices were mumbled coming from the verandah.

Etta was peering at Olivia watching her every move. She was eager to catch her doing anything that might be considered unladylike so that she could run to Jackson with the news. Olivia wouldn't mind starting a ruckus if it wouldn't upset her mother, that in turn would upset her father and that was one thing Olivia would never do. She leaned back on the edge of the windowsill with dreams flowing through her head as time ticked by slowly while everyone else around the room lay quietly in naiveté.

Mama Bea finally stood holding up the hem of her dress in her large hands, quietly moving over by Olivia.

"Child," she shook her head speaking softly. "Those green eyes is gwanna get youse in trouble," the old woman whispered, squeezing her mouth together. "Honey, youse jest be careful. I'z understands more than youse thinks. Now, here yo' dress."

Olivia jumped up from the window seat trying to be quiet. She reached over wrapping her arms around Mama Bea smiling at the old woman. She slipped on her beautiful dress quickly smoothing her hair.

"I will be careful, Mama Bea," Olivia whispered softly, straightening her dress. Etta sat not moving watching Olivia sneak through the room.

Olivia tiptoed past everyone as they quietly rested. She slowly crept down the stairs trying not to make any sound, but her body came to an abrupt stop before she made it to the bottom step. There to her astonishment was Jackson standing in the hallway near her father's office door. His eyes peeked up. She pulled in a deep breath. She had been caught. She quickly gathered her wits about her and descending the stairs with a more ladylike stride. Etta, hiding at the top of the stairs, watched Olivia transform and intuitively knew something was askew.

Jackson's boots echoed in the quiet hallway as he walked to the bottom of the staircase. He grinned up at Olivia believing she was on her way to find him.

He stepped up on the bottom step, "This is a wonderful surprise, my dear. Let's take a stroll. It is cooling down outside." His hand reached over taking her hand. "I do believe we will have some rain this evening."

Her ploy of seeing Andrew had backfired. She could see Benjamin looking out the office door shaking his head with compassion and then with amusement covering his face.

The band members were tuning up their instruments preparing for the dance. She knew the dance would begin soon and she would be saved from idle conversation with Jackson. The plantation was becoming alive with many people stirring and strolling around the massive grounds enjoying the beautiful gardens, and letting the peaceful silence vanish into the late afternoon.

The front door opened, William stepped out onto the verandah with Andrew close behind. They were followed by several men. William moved to the side of the veranda. He bowed as he greeted every person sitting around the splendid verandah. Andrew didn't stop; he continued on stepping down the steps out into the grounds. He distinguishably stood peering out onto the grand plantation taking everything in. His eyes turned toward Olivia and Jackson as they moved closer to him. Jackson softly slipped his arm around Olivia's tiny waist and led her over to Andrew.

"My dear, we haven't been formally introduced," the handsome young man said with the Northern accent, bowing to Olivia.

A smile came on his face. She remembered those blue eyes staring at her from the verandah earlier in the day.

"I'm Andrew Robert Drake."

Olivia held out her hand and he took her hand in his tenderly caressing her small hand.

"Andrew," Jackson began, "it is my pleasure to introduce, my fiancée, Miss Olivia Rose Bellamead."

"Yes, you are William's daughter, no denying that," Andrew smiled with the warmest smile. "Congratulations to the two of you."

"Maybe next spring you would be able to attend our wedding," Jackson said very proudly.

"I would be much honored," Andrew answered with his eyes telling a different story, still holding Olivia's hand gently.

Her body quivered. New feelings were overtaking her. The two stood silent, as he held onto her hand smiling down on her. His body snapped back into the gentleman stance as he realized how long they had been standing there. He reluctantly slid his hand away from hers and stepped back.

Guests began to congregate toward the band and migrate toward the dance floor. Etta made sure that she stood where she could watch Olivia. Just one wrong move; that was all she wanted to see.

The band began playing *Glory, Glory Hallelujah, Glory, Glory Hallelujah, Glory, Glory Hallelujah; His truth is marching on*, and the voices of the guests were ringing out the chorus across the grounds. Andrew stood next to Olivia with his wonderful baritone joining in the singing. She glanced up at him with a quick look and he smiled down on her with their eyes locking.

She looked out at all of the people standing preparing for the dance. The song ended and *Oh Susanna* began to play, the song the band had used her entire life to announce the beginning of the dance and for everyone to get ready.

There standing with his arm around her mother was her father with a warm smile, so jovial. She knew the love her parents had for each other. It might have been a socially correct marriage, but their love clearly could be seen when they looked at each other. The golden cross necklace that William had given Ruth for their anniversary this past spring glistened in the sun. Olivia sighed wishing she could have a marriage of love, instead of convenience, but that wasn't her destiny.

William and Ruth stepped up to dance when the *Grand March Medley* began. Their bodies twirled as one on the dance floor. Jackson reached over pulling Olivia with him to be the next couple following them. Everyone continued until the dance floor was filled.

The music continued with *Soldier's Joy Medley* beginning. Benjamin grabbed Annie and the two young people joined Jackson and Olivia with the fiddle playing and Annie laughing with her sweet innocent smile. The music slowly died and Jackson led Olivia off the platform. He bowed, leaving for a minute, to fetch a drink for her.

"Wasn't that grand," Annie called out to her sister trying to catch her breath.

"Yes, and your dancing has improved. Now, who have you been practicing dancing with young lady?" asked Olivia teasing her sister.

"Well, you ain't gonna tell on me?"

"No."

"Vincent Tolleson has been teaching me to dance when he comes over with his papa to work for Cyrus."

"Annie Bellamead, Mother would have a fit."

"But…he's so nice, not boring like *you know who*," she whispered with sympathy coming over her young face.

"Sweetie," Olivia sighed, "I hope you can follow your heart. I just wish I could."

"You're not married, yet," Annie smiled and eased away with Jackson stepping up.

"My daddy would like to talk to me for a few minutes. Will you be alright?" Jackson questioned.

"Of course'," Olivia sighed with relief, a reprieve for a little while. "I will be fine."

Jackson turned leaving her going over to the group of men under a large old oak.

Benjamin walked up. "Free, for a while, I see," he chuckled.

"For a while," Olivia assured.

"Not for long," Benjamin snickered, stepping back letting Andrew move close.

Andrew took her hand in his and once more gently caressing it. "Miss Olivia, may I have this dance?"

Her heart started hammering in her chest so loudly she was afraid he might hear as she tried to get her composure back.

"Yes," Benjamin said with a chuckle.

"Benjamin," Olivia scorned, nodding her head *yes* to Andrew.

Andrew led Olivia to the dance floor. The eyes of all the women were watching, but she did notice her father smiling as he stood to the side talking to some of the other plantation owners.

The music began to play *Virginia Reel Medley*. Andrew placed his right arm well around her waist clasping her fingers gently in his left hand and then placing her left hand tenderly on his right shoulder. She was in Heaven now looking up into his face. Andrew held onto her tightly whirling around, and she did not hold back her enthusiasm, either. She understood that she would probably be getting a talking to later that evening from her mother, but she was thrilled. She figured that her defense could be that she was seeing to one of their guests, as any good hostess would do. Then, she laughed to herself. The music continued and she hoped it would never end, but as all good things, the music stopped and Andrew bowed with a grin on his face.

"Thank you, my lady," he said kindly leading her to the side. "I'm sorry the dance had to end."

She nodded her head *yes*, hardly able to speak. She moved to the side away from the dance floor, still smiling with satisfaction. At that moment, she saw Etta standing to the side watching her like a hawk. The realization was more than she could take, knowing Jackson would be back and the passion she felt would be gone.

Chapter Four

"The Old Oak Tree"

Tears filled Olivia's eyes. She turned her head away from everyone trying discreetly to wipe them as they escaped. She hurriedly turned around and walked down to the path to her special hiding place, the one she had used since she was a young child. She entered into her extraordinary world with the cool air hitting her in the face taking away the droplets of perspiration on her forehead. The voices of all the people became quieter and quieter bringing a peaceful silence. The fresh scent of wild flowers blooming was floating in the soothing air.

She followed the winding path listening to the sound of the trickling water of the spring-fed Rock Creek flowing over the small waterfall calming her soul. Her long dress brushed the grass swishing back and forth. She stopped walking and stared down at the swimming hole in the sparkling creek, the one the family used on hot summer days, like today, except when no one was around. The trees were entwined like umbrellas, hiding the sun's warmth. The birds were singing overhead telling their tales.

She sat down on the ground next to one of the old, twisted oak trees not worrying about her beautiful dress. She leaned back against the trunk of the tree closing her eyes listening to the water gently flow over the large rocks. She was lost in her dreams of what her life could be. Tears flowed down her face understanding she was to marry Jackson next spring.

A noise startled her. She heard boots crunching the dried leaves. She wiped the wetness from her cheeks. Her damp green eyes peered down her path seeing a tall silhouette of someone coming near. She took in a deep breath of air believing Jackson had found her.

"My dear, I hope I'm not intruding," came from a sweet familiar voice.

She looked up into the kind caring face peering down on her. Her lips curled into a smile, studying those blue eyes. Andrew crouched beside her, each knowing the consequences of his being alone with a young Southern girl.

"No, not at all. It is so pleasant and cool down here," she answered quickly, wiping her eyes not wanting him to see her tears.

"Benjamin let me know this is where you were headed."

"I love to come down here and think and get away from everyone."

"I shall leave if you would like? I didn't mean to interfere with your time alone."

"No," she responded reaching up to him wrapping her fingers around his arm before he could leave. "Please join me."

"Your fiancé wouldn't be happy."

She grinned up at him, "Why did you come here to see Father? Isn't it dangerous for you?" she asked, curiously.

"Yes," He leaned over near her as he played with a blade of grass. "My father sent me to warn your father about the Union Army and the war."

"Did he listen to you?"

"No, he is a stubborn man, I see…like you," he answered, with his eyes squinted stroking his chin with his other hand.

"Why would your father risk your life for you to warn my father?" she asked tilting her head taking in every aspect of the young man sitting next to her.

"My father John and your father grew up together and came here from England years ago. Your father stayed here in South Carolina, and my father, a surgeon, moved to Philadelphia. Your father has helped my father with legal problems over the years and they have been and always will be best friends, as close as brothers."

"Then you would be my cousin, I would presume," she said raising one eyebrow.

He chuckled, shrugging his shoulders, shaking his head back and forth.

"I don't remember your father ever coming to visit us," she added.

"No, he hasn't ever been to Bella Oak," Andrew paused taking in a deep breath. "Not long after I was born, he was thrown by a horse and paralyzed and isn't able to travel. It is a shame he has always wished to visit Bella Oak Plantation, and William and Ruth. The trip would be too tiring for him. His accident is what made me want to go to medical school to become a surgeon like him. I had to learn and understand more about what happened to my father."

"Oh, I'm sorry about your father," she added looking up into his eyes tilting her head to the side. "You do look like a medical doctor."

"Your father," Andrew leaned back on his hands, "has visited us many times, and I learned when I was a young boy what a good man he really is. And, a good friend, too."

"The war…isn't going to be easy, is it?" she questioned looking at his worried face.

"No, and I'm troubled. The men here are so stubborn like your father not understanding the dire straits that they are putting themselves in."

She moaned not wanting to take life seriously.

"My dear, you don't need to worry your pretty head. Your father is a wise man," he assured, leaning in close to her.

"Benjamin wants to join the Confederates," she bit her lip gazing up at him. "Will you be joining the Union? Oh my, then you would be fighting against each other," slowly shaking her head. "This is so strange."

"I'm not planning on fighting, but," he moaned leaning his head back, "enough talk of the war."

Her eyes took every movement in as he lay back in the grass with the sun flickering through the thick branches shining down dancing on him.

He took a deep breath and enjoyed the fresh sweet smell of spring water, "This is so nice down here. I should have stayed down here the whole day away from prying eyes."

"Yes, it is wonderful. I would love to stay awhile, but I will have to be getting back."

"No," he grinned looking up through the trees listening to the birds sing, "you don't have to hurry. Your brother told Jackson you weren't feeling well and needed to rest for a while."

Andrew rolled over on his side close to her with his head resting in his hand looking at her green eyes so full of liveliness.

"He cares for you," Andrew assured.

"Benjamin," she shook her head in agreement. "He knows how much I love it down here, along with our tree."

"Tree," he quickly sat up.

"Our old tree, across the creek," she declared, "the one that is up stream."

"Will you show me?"

"Sure, I will," she beamed.

He stood up and reached his hand to her gently pulling her near him, looking down on her only inches apart, neither one moving.

"This way," she finally said and turned from him. Lifting her long dress way above her ankles, she stepped on the rocks carefully crossing the creek with Andrew following close behind her. They made their way to the other side of the bank, dashing up a small hill.

"This plantation is so lovely," he tightened his lips. "I grew up in the city…nothing like this." He stopped walking. "Oh! This is so peaceful…" he whispered, not finishing his sentence trying to take everything in around him.

"I couldn't live in town. I have to be free. I want to live here on Bella Oak the rest of my life."

"That…I would love," he added tenderly ducking his head down to the ground not looking her in the eyes. She turned back smiling at him scrunching her eyes with a questioning look.

He hurriedly continued up the hill, but abruptly stopped walking, "My Lord, that is the most gorgeous tree I have ever seen."

He hurried past her over to the old gnarled oak tree with a few of its colossal branches lying gently on the ground, and its other limbs spreading out canopying over their heads. "Oh, the tree is welcoming us into its world. This is so wonderful," he spun around looking up through the branches. She lifted her dress up with her underskirt showing. Then she stepped up on a large bottom limb that was lying on the ground. She reached her hand up to a large branch above pulling herself onto limb after limb.

"Now, don't tell anyone what I'm doing," she pleaded settling in on the massive limb allowing her dress to fall down around her.

He grinned amused, "Your secret is safe with me."

His hands gripped the limb above him. Swinging his body up to the next limb, he scooted close to her on her limb. He ducked his head down near her.

"However, next time, let me assist you," Andrew teased.

She smiled leaning back against another limb.

"Look, you can see down onto a waterfall!" he exclaimed with his excitement growing.

"Yes, and if you climb higher, you can see to the river and over to the plantation home."

"Will they spot me if I go up there to the top of the tree?" he questioned anxiously, squirming like a young boy.

"No, if you don't wiggle too much," she laughed. "It would be hard to see you from the plantation, unless someone happened to be looking for you."

He reached his hand up grabbing the large limb above him pulling his body up limb after limb until he was at the top of the massive tree. His shadow swayed down on her shading her from the sun. She leaned back peering up at him. He sat, not moving, staring so far out toward the river, so enthralled.

"The dance is still going on. I don't think anyone will miss us. I'm sure Benjamin has been busy," he added laughing with his enthusiasm becoming infectious.

"Oh, I wish I could move up there with you, but I might tear my dress and Mother would be furious."

"No, we don't need that. Maybe next time," he announced, peering down on her assuring her he would be back another time.

"I do hope so," she glanced up at him with her face becoming flushed hoping he didn't notice as she put her hand up in front of her face.

He zigzagged his way down the branches. The limbs creaked with a few small twigs falling from the huge tree. He gently lifted her dress to the side scooting in close to her on her limb.

"You have moss and leaves all over you," she laughed wiping his arms off as he continued to stare.

"You don't care for Jackson Montgomery, do you?" he asked brazenly.

"My, you come to the point," she chuckled. "Our marriage is an arranged marriage."

"I see. I don't have much time here, so that is why I must waste no time with silly mundane questions."

"I like that," her eyes were being drawn to his. "When will you be leaving?"

"In the morning," he answered with his eyebrows furrowing and his lips tightening.

"You can't stay longer…" she bowed her head playing with some moss.

She knew she wasn't acting properly. A lady would never do or say such things to a young man she had just met. She turned her head. She wasn't able to look in his eyes; she was afraid he would be able to see into her soul.

"If I could stay, I would, but it is getting more dangerous to travel each day and I have to get back to see to my father."

His hand reached over gently touching her chin, lifting her face to him. He smiled down on her with more on his mind, "But, maybe I should have a talk with William."

"Oh, this war," her arms flew into the air. "I wish they would settle it and everything go back the way it was."

"My dear," he declared, "you, and everyone else."

Her eyes looked up into those blue eyes fixed on her.

"The music is so nice echoing up the hill. Would you like to dance?" he asked.

"Yes," she said nervously, he was so different from the boys she had been around, a man not a boy. He had so much confidence and stated what was on his mind.

He climbed down from the tree putting his hands on her waist lifting her from their limb. He held onto her for a few seconds longer caressing her. Andrew then took her hand in his leading her over to a shaded spot. He put his arm around her waist and held her tightly. They began to spin under the old oak tree. Her face gently rested on his chest. She could feel him breathing. She was closer than a lady should be, but she didn't care. She tilted her head back with her eyes peering up into his eyes understanding she had fallen in love.

His head leaned down with their lips meeting, each knowing this wasn't proper behavior for a young lady or gentleman. As the music flowed, her dress swirled. Her emotions grew into passionate love. She knew now she would never marry Jackson, no matter what life would bring.

Andrew smiled down on her as if he could read her mind. The music ended, so he stopped dancing.

"No," she protested, "I don't want to leave."

"My dear, they will be sending out a search party for us and the men here are ready as it is to string me up for being a Yankee. They sure can't catch me with a young Southern lady all alone away from everyone."

"I don't want to leave," she swallowed, biting her lower lip.

"I will meet you later tonight in William's office after everyone is asleep. You, my dear, straighten yourself up and join the festivities and I will join them later."

He held onto her and pulled her close. She reached up pulling his face near, kissing him again. She didn't say the words out loud only in her mind, "I love you."

His hands fell to his side stepping back letting her go, but she could see that he yearned to grab her and tell her not to leave. She gradually moved away leaving him standing by the tree, still feeling his stare. She held her dress up high away from the water. Her feet carefully stepped onto the rocks crossing the flowing creek. She stopped on the other side of the creek, straightened her dress, and puffed up her hair, being sure she was proper. She tried to smooth her rumpled dress with her hands, but it wasn't helping. Little by little, she made her way up through the trees and up the hill to the side of the massive home.

Benjamin was standing over to the side and saw her. He quickly ran to her side taking her arm and walking back up the hill with her. Jackson was standing alone with a bored look on his face. When he spotted Olivia, he quickly hurried over to her.

"I see, Olivia, you are feeling better," Jackson said with relief. "Benjamin I will see to her now, thank you."

She smiled up at Jackson, but thinking only of Andrew. Etta was standing over to the side near the dance floor. Olivia's body ached, wishing she could run over and tell Etta to pursue Jackson all she wanted. How she wanted to be free of Jackson! But, she couldn't disrupt the happy mood of the picnic. Olivia resolved that there would be another time.

Chapter Five

"Having to Say Goodbye"

Jackson continued to hold onto Olivia's arm as he began his tales about his plantation and the plans he had for the two of them when they were married. She wished she was able to reach up and stop his mouth so she could let him know she would never marry him.

"Olivia," he whispered in a caring voice, leaning down close to her, "would you like to dance? There are only a few more dances left?"

"Yes," she answered with guilt overcoming her.

Jackson led them to the dance floor. Voices disappeared from around the grounds with quietness coming over Bella Oak as they danced. Fathers lifted tired children into carriages getting ready to leave after a long day of celebration.

William stood to the side shaking the men's hands as families walked past him out to the buggies. With each turn on the dance floor, Olivia continued to look down the path to the spring creek. She shivered.

Andrew with his head bowed was taking short strides moving up the hill from the spring slowly swishing a small stick in front of him. He looked up seeing Olivia. She smiled back at him. A smile finally emerged on his troubled face.

Jackson leaned in next to her softly whispering, "My dear, this is our final dance." Jackson's hand reached around her pulling her close.

To her surprise, Andrew walked up to the dance floor. He stood so properly. He gently reached over taking Annie's small hand.

"Miss Annie Bellamead, would you do me the honor of dancing with me for the last dance at Bella Oak?"

Annie blushed and answered in a nervous whisper, "Yes," as she looked over at Olivia.

Olivia smiled back at her younger sister and Andrew. Now that the evening was ending beautifully, she wasn't thinking about Jackson holding her. The music became soft, fading into the air.

Jackson's arm stayed around her waist leading her over to the verandah.

He leaned in with such considerate eyes, "My dear, I see you are tired."

"Yes," she assured, "I guess staying up last night and this full day has been more tiring than I presumed, but this has been the most marvelous picnic we have ever had."

"My dear, I agree. I will leave, let you rest, and I will call on you soon."

"Good bye, Jackson," she said. He leaned down and softly kissed her on the cheek.

She turned and stepped up onto the verandah and walked over near Andrew and Benjamin. The evening was bringing with it darkness. They watched Jackson ride his strong, grey horse down the long path and disappear through the gates of Bella Oak.

Olivia grabbed hold of her brother. She pulled him close giving him a hug, whispering *thank you*. She reached up touching his thoughtful face not having to say anything else.

"Now," he said, grinning like a Cheshire cat, "I understand, tonight I will be on alert again."

She nodded her head, *yes*.

William with the biggest smile stepped up onto the verandah, "This I have dreamed of that my children and John's would become friends. I jest wish my friend could be here and see your faces. My son, you should have come to visit sooner."

"I concur, William. Your family has been very kind," Andrew assured.

Benjamin snickered and Olivia punched him in the side not letting her father see.

"It is getting' late and I'm shor' Ruth is tired, so I will say goodnight. I know Mama Bea and my children will see to your comforts."

"Good night, William and again thank you for your hospitality," Andrew answered shaking hands.

Olivia looped Andrew's arm in hers.

"Father said we are to see to you," she added grinning, leading him inside the home.

There standing to the back of the foyer was Mama Bea watching. They were caught.

Andrew leaned down squeezing her hand and whispered, "I will be in the office when you are free. Don't rush and don't let anyone see you."

"Good night, Andrew," she said kindly letting her arm slip from his.

"Good night, Miss Olivia," he nodded bending over bowing. "It has been my pleasure to meet such a lovely lady and talk with you. It was a wonderful afternoon that I shall long remember."

He followed Benjamin to William's office. He stopped before going through the door glancing back at Olivia. Then, he looked over at Mama Bea's steely eyes watching him. Mama Bea walked up next to Olivia. She didn't have to say anything. A young lady shouldn't be left alone without a chaperon when an unmarried gentleman was in the home, so she followed Olivia upstairs to her room.

Olivia opened her bedroom door and went to her bed. Annie slipped off her beautiful dress and quickly tugged on her nightgown. Olivia handed her beautiful dress with grass stains to Mama Bea. Those dark eyes of Mama Bea's studied the rumpled dress and the dirty hem line; she tightened her mouth. Olivia turned her face from Mama Bea hiding her grin. She slipped on her nightgown and lay down in her bed.

"I see, child, that yo's tired." Mama Bea said as she folded the dress laying it over her arm. She walked over tucking quilts around both girls even in the warmth of the night.

"Yes, I'm tired. This has been a long day," Olivia answered closing her eyes.

"Good night," Mama Bea said in a low voice closing the door. The house was becoming quiet.

"This picnic was so wonderful, today was perfect," Annie proclaimed pushing the quilt off of her turning and lying on her side propping her head up with the large feather pillow.

"Annie, is there more to the day that you want to share with me?"

"Yes," she blushed, sitting up in her bed, "Vincent Tolleson showed up for the dance and we danced to the wonderful music back behind the ole smoke house. It was marvelous," she insisted, humming to the music of the day.

She fell back down on her bed, as if she was swooning making Olivia laugh. Maybe Annie was the real Southern belle for Bella Oak.

"Young lady, do we need to talk?"

"No, don't be silly," Annie giggled, "I just love to dance and Vincent is so kind and caring."

Olivia shook her head, grinning, "I did hear Andrew bragging on how elegantly you danced. That was quite a compliment from a refined gentleman."

"I was so scared dancing with him. He did make me feel so at ease from the moment we began to dance. He is very nice, but I see in your eyes, you already know that about him."

"Don't you tell a soul, Annie," Olivia said, giving her a stern look.

"I won't. I guess we both have secrets to keep and I won't tell anyone, I promise...." Annie got quiet, "I'm jest sorry..." Annie looked over at her sister with her eyes sinking gazing downward, "that Andrew is leaving so soon."

"He will be back. He promised, and a gentleman never goes back on his promises," Olivia said convincingly with tears building.

"Alright, what else is going on?"

"Since you know my secret," she hesitated, "I'm meeting Andrew downstairs in the office after everyone is asleep."

"Well, what are you waiting on? Fix your bed; here's an extra pillow to stuff under the quilts."

An extra pillow landed on Olivia's bed.

Annie giggled, "In case Mama Bea checks on us."

"Thank you, Annie."

"Hurry up and get dressed your wasting precious time."

Olivia slipped her everyday dress on and hid her sleeping clothes under the cover with the tail end hanging out.

"There, that looks like I'm sleeping, doesn't it?"

"Yes, that'll do fine."

Olivia pulled on the quilt one last time.

"Benjamin is in on this too, isn't he?"

"Yes, he helped me sneak down by the spring with Andrew."

"Well, get going and be careful," Annie waved her arm toward the door.

Annie lay back in her bed pulling the quilt over her head snuggling. Her eyes closed dreaming of her own life.

Olivia slowly opened their bedroom door peeking out into the long hallway. All was quiet. She stepped down the stairs with her bare feet on the cool floor quietly making it to the foyer.

The house was still with the only sound coming from the ticking of the old grandfather clock in the foyer. The light in the office was glowing from under the door. She reached over and gently turned the doorknob pushing the door open.

Andrew was standing facing the window. She stepped quietly into the room, but he heard her and turned around. He hurried over, softly closed the door taking her in his arms.

"The time seemed to move so slowly when I'm waiting for you, but when we are together, it spins out of control."

He pulled her face up to his kissing her with so much desire. There just wasn't time for appropriate protocol.

"I see the storm is moving in," she whispered.

She moved over by the window watching the lightning grow brighter out in the dark sky with the flashes of lightning illuminating the room every few minutes revealing their troubled faces.

"Yes, the storm will cover the sounds of our voices. God is even helping us have time alone," he added trying to smile.

"The rain will be here soon and that always puts everyone to sleep."

"I don't think I will be able to sleep tonight," he answered staring down at her.

She turned from the window looking back into those blue eyes she never wanted to forget.

"It is very dangerous for you to ride home tomorrow, isn't it?"

"Yes, but you shouldn't worry so. I will be fine," he answered wrapping his arm around her with passion growing.

"I overheard your conversation out on the verandah with Father when you arrived."

"Oh, a spy, and what, my lady, did you hear that has you so worried?"

He softly pushed back her long flowing hair from her face.

"That the Union and Confederate Armies are already fighting in Virginia and you have to travel that way."

She closed her eyes for a second feeling his soft touch, the hands of a surgeon.

"I'm planning on staying away from the coast; it seems the battles are near there."

He ducked his head down with anxiety not able to hide his concern.

"For now, I'll be safe."

"You will write me and tell me you made it home safely."

"Benjamin and I have already thought about that. I will send him your letters and he has promised to be a gentleman and not read our private words to each other. Do you trust him?"

"Benjamin is a man of his word and I trust him more than anyone in my life."

"Well now, I will have to fix that," he assured, pulling her even closer. "I hope you will trust and believe in me one day."

"I hope someday…" her voice trailed off not finishing her sentence as she wiped a lone tear running down her face.

"My dear, there will be a someday for us," he paused taking in a deep breath, "Miss Olivia Rose Bellamead, I can't actually ask you to marry me, since you are engaged," he chuckled. "But I will anyway, you know I don't hold back. So, Miss Olivia Rose Bellamead," he began, getting down on one knee, "will you marry me when I come back to Bella Oak?"

"Yes, Mr. Andrew Robert Drake, I would be honored." She smiled putting her hands in his, pulling him back up. "Now, you have to be a gentleman and come back and fulfill your promise."

"Then, you also understand, you will have to break your engagement with Jackson, a lady shouldn't be engaged to two men at once," he grinned.

"My dear, this will make the biggest stir that the folks around here have ever heard tell of."

"I surely won't be welcomed here after everyone finds out you plan to marry a Yankee."

"You will always be welcomed at Bella Oak and this will be your plantation to live on. You won't have to be a city boy after we are married, but you will have a lot to learn."

He grabbed her squeezing her tight.

"We will have the rest of our lives for me to learn. I don't have a ring, but I do have something for you to show I'm a gentleman and my word is good."

He pulled out a gold chain with a small charm and a ruby stone in the middle. Gently, he lifted her hand up laying the sparkling chain in her palm.

"This is beautiful, where did you get it?"

"That is a charm my father gave my mother when I was born," his words seemed to choke him, but he recovered his emotions. As he gently wiped his eyes, "My mother died when I was nine, and she gave me this necklace for good luck a few days before she died, telling me she would always be with me."

Olivia stared down at the charm, knowing how difficult this must be for him to give it away.

"Andrew, I know you're a man of your word and you should keep this."

"No," he said with so much affection, lifting the gold chain up closing the clasp around her neck, "this is yours and I will see it when I return for your hand in marriage." Her hand softly touched the charm knowing she would never take it off. They kissed again.

"So, tell me about growing up in the city," she questioned.

She took his arm and moved over to the chairs in the back of the room as the thunder grew shaking the plantation home.

"Do you have any brothers or sisters?"

"No, it is only me. You are very lucky to have siblings. It was lonely growing up…and our house," he sighed, "after Mother died…became too quiet."

"I wouldn't know how to act without my brothers and sister. Oh and, thank you for dancing with Annie. She was thrilled, and by the way, she does know about us too."

Olivia moved from the chair sitting down on the floor, staring at the cold fireplace in front of her. Andrew kneeled down by her. She pulled him close with his arms wrapping around her as they snuggle. Her emotions were taking over again. She had never felt the passion she felt with Andrew. She wanted to remember those feelings while Andrew was away until the day he would return to Bella Oaks to marry her.

"It seems our secret isn't much of a secret anymore. Oh, you will have to write and tell me tales about growing up here on this massive plantation with your siblings. Knowing family stories will make me feel closer to you."

Tears welled up in her eyes and began to flow down her face.

"I have known you a day and it feels like my entire life. I will worry every day until you come home to me. This war…."

He leaned in kissing her, "Please don't worry so. I will send a letter."

The thunder boomed making her shake and he held her close as they nestled, each recognizing the fact that they might never see each other again. The time sped on just as he had said. Five o'clock bonged on the old grandfather clock in the foyer with eeriness in the silence of the night. Andrew sighed lifting up her sweet face.

"I must go and prepare for my journey and you, my dear, should go to your room. It won't be any easier if we wait until the last second until I leave. Please remember, I love you and will always love you," he said, taking her hand, standing, and pulling her up to him.

He hugged her as they kissed their one last kiss. He reached down touching her lips with his finger.

"I would like to remember everything about you. I love you, my dear."

"I will always love you, Andrew," she whispered.

Her hand turned the doorknob and she carefully peered out into the foyer. She turned and looked back into the office seeing Andrew standing by the widow.

She made it to her room. She settled into her sleeping gown dreaming of the life she hoped to have. Mama Bea came into the room and she closed her eyes.

"Miss Olivia, it's six o'clock and Mr. Andrew is preparing to leave. Yo' father would like youse to say goodbye."

"Yes," Olivia stretched, "I do wish to say goodbye... and I have to get dressed."

"Child, did yo' not sleep well. Yo face is drawn."

"I'm jest very tired, but I'll be fine," Olivia assured, slipping on her dress, ready to go downstairs.

It was like walking in mud down the stairs not knowing if she could say goodbye. She wanted to hold onto Andrew and not let him go. She could hear voices coming from her father's office. She walked up and Benjamin and Andrew were talking with her father. Benjamin looked over at her sad face.

"Father, I have a question. May I talk to you for a minute in private out in the foyer?" Benjamin requested.

"Yes, excuse me for a second, Andrew," William smiled, "Olivia will keep you company."

Andrew stepped up putting his arms around her kissing her.

"Olivia, this isn't goodbye. We will never say goodbye. I will see you soon. I love you."

"I love you, too," she sniffed stepping back wiping her eyes when the door opened.

Benjamin and her father stepped in and she turned her face from them.

"Son, you must to be on your way," William offered shaking hands, and then grabbing the young man's shoulder. "Tell your father when all of this war is over I will be up to see him."

He sighed seeing his old friend in the young man's face. It brought back memories of his childhood.

"I will sir," Andrew added, "and if you need my help, let me know."

He looked over at Olivia. The two men walked out onto the verandah along with Benjamin. The morning sun was glowing in the east, and was making a fresh beginning for the new day after the thunderstorm the night before. Jonas brought Andrew's huge black horse with a white tipped face. Andrew leaped up into the saddle.

"God's speed and may He keep you safe, my son," called out William waving his arm.

"God keep you and your family safe, as well. Goodbye Sir," Andrew shouted back taking one more look at Olivia.

He kicked the side of the horse riding off down the path. The young man slowed down at the entrance looking back at the massive plantation. He gripped the horse's reins, knowing the odds of war weren't good, but hoping someday to be back.

Benjamin ducked his head trying to hold back his emotions. He turned quickly going inside the home. He understood how treacherous the ride home would be for Andrew. Olivia turned to follow Benjamin still trying to hide her face, not allowing her father to see her cry.

Then, William stepped in front of her. He lifted up her face seeing tears flowing down. He looked into her sad green eyes so much like his.

"Alright, young lady, we need to talk," he compassionately smiled down on her.

"Father…" she choked with her throat squeezing so tight that she was unable to talk.

He wrapped his arms around her, "I see. Andrew was only here for one day, but he made an impact."

She nodded her head *yes*.

"How close did you two become?" he asked still peering into those sad eyes.

"I fell in love with him and he asked me to marry him when he comes back."

"My goodness, the boy works fast," he concluded tilting his head smiling, "but I can't say a word, I fell in love with your mother the first time I saw her."

"Mother is going to be so upset with me," she sobbed. "I have ruined everything for her."

"Oh, I don't think so," William said as he gradually turned Olivia's head to the side.

"Mother," Olivia cried, running over to her, "I didn't want to hurt you."

"Your father and I were talking last night before we went to sleep about how strange love can be. We could see how your face lit up around Andrew, and we were almost certain that your engagement to Jackson was not what you really want. You don't have to explain to us. What you don't know about your father and me," Ruth exhaled, "is that I was engaged to be married to a man from Charleston when I met William. I guess it runs in the family to fall in love with someone else when you're engaged, but I chose love and so shall you."

"That being said, I'm going to leave you ladies to talk. I am going to have a talk with my son," laughed William, "I'm shor' he had his hand in this."

"Father," Olivia urged reaching out her hand to her father, "please, don't punish Benjamin. This was all my doing. Benjamin just put my happiness first."

"Honey, I would never punish Benjamin for being loyal to you," he answered patting her hand. "I jest want to stir him up," he laughed.

He stopped walking, "Honey, you look worried; we're not upset with you."

"I understand, but Father, this war…and Andrew is a Northerner who has to ride through Virginia." Tears began to flow, "Andrew might not be back."

He nodded his head slowly agreeing without a verbal answer. Ruth wrapped her arms around Olivia.

"Sweetie, we will jest have to pray each day that he will come back to you," she sighed squeezing her daughter.

She led her into the house.

"You must have been up most of the night. You go upstairs to your room, get some rest, and we will talk later."

Olivia nodded her head *yes*. She lifted her dress stepping slowly up the stairs. She stopped and peered down at her mother. Ruth smiled up at her.

The twinge in Olivia's heart wouldn't let up. She lifted her head and said softly into the breath of the morning, "Andrew, I love you. Please come home to me.

Chapter Six

"Joining the Confederate Army"

The next few days moved on slowly with news of the war increasing as battles were being fought all over the South. The news continued of additional battles in Virginia causing Olivia more distress. It was so difficult for her to hear the tales of fighting. Hot sweltering, summer days continued without any word from Andrew or Jackson.

Jackson had been busy at his plantation and hadn't visited, so there hadn't been a chance for her to sit down with him and talk. As time moved on, the looming and inevitable job of breaking off her engagement concerned her. This late July day was humid and sweltering hot.

Olivia sat on the verandah knitting listening to music flowing from the open windows behind her as Annie played the piano in the parlor. She could see dust flowing in the air and a lone rider coming up the path.

She took a deep breath seeing it was Jackson. She lay the knitting down on a table and stood. She had practiced repeatedly in her mind what to say to him, but now her mind had gone blank.

"Olivia," he called out jumping down off his strong grey horse loaded with saddlebags.

He turned to Terrance.

"Terrance, please keep my horse close, I shall be leaving soon," Jackson called out, handing the boy the reins.

Jackson stepped up onto the verandah and lifted his hat off twirling it in his hands. He was standing confidently in front of Olivia as he stepped up on the verandah.

She started to talk. "Jackson…"

He interrupted, "Olivia, my dear, I don't have much time. However, I had to see you one last time."

"Jackson, what are you saying?"

The music stopped inside. Annie walked to the window always a spy.

"I'm on my way to Savannah. I have joined the Confederate Army, and my orders are to meet with my troop immediately."

"No!" she cried out. "This war! This can't be happening." She grabbed hold of his arm, "Why would you do such a thing?"

"I have to fight to save our land. We can't have those Yankees come and take us over."

"No!" she shouted, her head shook back and forth. "You can't leave," she cried out as her thoughts ended softly, "…too."

He cupped her arm in his pulling her close.

"I will write you, my dear Olivia, and I will be home shortly. Our army is growing stronger each day. The war will end soon and the South will be free to live as we please."

William stepped out the door onto the verandah along with Benjamin. They stared at Jackson seeing the disturbing look on Olivia's face.

"Sir," Jackson began letting go of Olivia, walking toward William. "I'm leaving for Savannah, joining the troops of Colonel Charles Olmstead," Jackson proclaimed with excitement.

William shook his head. He looked at Olivia wondering what she would say.

"My son, may the almighty Lord keep you safe," he said shaking Jackson's hand.

William's head bent down. The war had come close to home.

Benjamin stepped up, "I will be joining the Confederate Army soon and I will see you on the battlefield, Jackson."

"I'm not the only one around these parts to join. We have a group that is meeting in the square in town to ride to Savannah. Albert and Hansford Tolleson are leaving too, along with Lawrence Dawson and Jerrold Baxter," he stepped near Olivia, "and a few others from some small farms to the west of us."

Her face tense, Olivia didn't move, not knowing what to say. Words wouldn't come.

"Benjamin, our group is large enough right now to leave to go fight. You, son," he took in a deep breath turning to Benjamin, "please stay and protect our homes and families."

Jackson patted young Benjamin on the back giving him a strong look of trust.

"My dear, we will all be home soon," Jackson assured. Leaning in kissing her on the cheek, "I will be back for our wedding; that I promise." He smiled down on her and put his hat back on, descended the steps, and waved goodbye as he climbed back upon his strong steed riding off.

"Olivia, are you alright?" William pulled her near, holding onto his daughter. Tears ran down her face.

"I couldn't break his heart, Father, not as he goes off to war! I'm sorry, I just couldn't."

He wiped the tears from her face, "You did right."

He turned to Benjamin who was fidgeting behind him, "Son, you aren't joining the Confederates. You're too young, so don't give me that look. I know you are capable of fighting, but someone has to stay here and defend Bella Oak."

"But, Father, it's time for me to join the troops with the rest of my friends."

"Not yet, son, not yet," William said in a low voice as he turned.

Walking toward the door with his shoulders drooping, William left the two young people standing on the verandah. The atmosphere became solemn. This war was affecting every aspect of life, and it wasn't someone else's war. William agonized over his decision to stay on and not leave Bella Oak. Maybe John had been right; maybe he should have left with his family for England.

Weeks move on and no word from Andrew. Olivia spent all of her time working around the plantation trying to stay busy. Everyone was walking on eggshells not wanting to discuss Andrew with her, except Benjamin. He could never hold back.

The afternoon of August thirtieth, 1861, Olivia heard a ruckus in the front yard. She saw Terrance a young slave about Benjamin's age, running to give Benjamin something. Benjamin clasped his hands as if it were a piece of gold with a huge smile on his face.

He hopped up the verandah steps, yelling, "Olivia, Olivia!"

She ran out the front door onto the verandah. William followed close behind her. Benjamin handed her an envelope with the distinguish writing of Andrew addressed to Benjamin. Her hands shook with tears building.

"He made it home," she kept saying studying the return address.

She sat down in one of the chairs on the verandah. Benjamin and William stood near with concern growing in their faces.

"Here," she handed each of them a page, "these are your letters."

DIARY OF OLIVIA BELLAMEAD

She sat quietly in the smoldering heat of the August afternoon as Benjamin began to read his letter out loud:

Saturday, August second, 1861

My young friend,

I have to first thank you for your support. You are a fine confidant and hopefully, someday a brother. Your loyalty is a great attribute of a fine gentleman. I suppose you are still willing to join the Confederates. I beg you to reconsider. This note is for your eyes only, not for your sister's.

I have witnessed the beginning of the war on my journey home. I, a bystander for the moment, lent a hand with the wounded of the confrontation between the Union and Confederacy at Manassas, Virginia. There were so many wounded and mangled. My mind still cannot comprehend seeing all those young lads with missing legs and arms that had been severed by the battlefield surgeon on the battlefield. The fear on their faces will stay with me forever, as they looked up at me while I put clean dressings on their wounds preparing them for the long train ride home.

These were good men, farmers, growers, and store owners, not trained soldiers. Many never had been away from home before. They surely weren't the enthusiastic men who had left for war.

Now, they lie quietly in disbelief. I just pray that they make it home alive. Infection is widespread among the war wounded.

Then, my young friend, the dead showed up being transported to train cars to be shipped home as cattle. The stench of the dead was horrible and the body count continued on and on. They passed by me in wagons with bodies stacked six high.

This I wish my mind could erase, but I shall live with the image the rest of my life. I dare say, I didn't see the Confederate wounded, but heard horror stories of the likes.

I once more beg you, Benjamin, please stay on Bella Oak and keep the plantation safe along with my Olivia. This war, my young friend, will not end well.

Your friend,
Andrew

"Oh, I probably shouldn't have read the letter out loud," Benjamin said somberly. "Sorry, but Olivia, it's important that we understand."

William nodded his head agreeing with his son. He lifted up his letter and began to read:

Saturday, August second, 1861

My dear Friend,

I am writing this along with my father, John. First, he wishes you well. He has been working much too hard at the hospital, but as you know, he is obstinate. It is so hard on him to get around, but he won't give up.

He does miss your visits. He hopes the war will be over soon and you two will be able to sit and talk of old times and sip a glass of scotch together.

My journey home was one I won't ever forget in my entire life. As I feared, the war has escalated and the state of Virginia is becoming stained with the blood of young men. The battlefield of Bull Run, Manassas of Virginia became a bloody field that I alone did not witness but atrocities are emerging in stories.

I did witness the wounded and dead understanding the grim tales of battle are true. Brigadier General Irvin McDowell marched with his strong army from Washington to gain control of the railroad at Manassas. Brigadier General P.G.T. Beauregard and his men defended their post. It seemed, though both armies were ready to fight, they were not prepared for battle.

Even though the victory went to the Confederates, when it ended, over a hundred young men's lives were lost, and in my eyes, I see no victory. I chose to become a doctor to heal, but I say I have seen more wounded and dead in the past month than I ever expected to see in a lifetime.

I am worried for your family with the news of the North marching southward. I do regret to announce that I have also been summoned to join the Union Army as a medical officer, as a surgeon. It seems I will be leaving my father immediately and will be on active duty in a number of small hospitals close to the battlefields, equipping them with supplies at least for a while.

Then, I regret to add, I will be departing to join an active artillery troop. Being young, I will not stay in the hospitals long to take care of the wounded. I will leave that up to my father and his associates.

I will do my best to keep my letters coming. William, I had hoped to tell you in person, but alas, that might not come true.

I have fallen deeply in love with your daughter, Olivia. We were to keep our love silent until I returned, but I cannot withhold my feelings.

I shall, on my return to Bella Oak, by the grace of God, marry her. I trust and dearly hope with your blessing.

I so anticipate the day of my return. Please, Sir, keep my beloved protected for one of us in jeopardy is enough. May God keep you and your family safely in His care.

Your friend,

Andrew Drake and my father John

Olivia sat there in her chair crying. This was so difficult hearing that Andrew would be out in the battles and that so many men had already lost their lives. Benjamin tilted his head down walking down the steps out into the yard not looking back. William bent down softly stroking his daughter long, curly brown hair. He kissed her on the forehead leaving her alone to read her letter in private.

The door closed with a squeak in the silence and she picked up the paper with her hand trembling:

Saturday, August second, 1861

My dearest Olivia, my precious love,

I, at last, am safe for now with my father at his home back in Philadelphia sitting here out of harm's way in my bedroom. My body aches to hold you as we did the night before I left. I will always have the memories of that night, sitting down by the spring creek, and dancing with you under the old twisted oak. The memories are in my mind of how your soft skin felt as I caressed you, the scent of your hair, the fullness of your lips.

My father beamed with happiness when I told him about us. He couldn't hide his excitement at the thought of seeing you for the first time. When I conveyed your beauty, he smiled with a smile that I hadn't seen in years.

It seems your father had a sister two years younger than he, named Olivia. She must have been the spitting image of you.

When my father spoke of her, I could see there was more to their friendship than was ever told. He talked of her long, brown curly hair and those green eyes, just as yours.

However, as many love stories go, in the end Olivia died when she was fifteen, devastating William and my father.

I imagine in your face even from this distance you are worried about my travels. I did happen upon some wounded soldiers from a battle and gave assistance. My dear, this war is horrifying and I hope you will not have to witness any of it.

I have asked Benjamin to stay and protect you and Bella Oak. I pray he will continue on as a protector and never leave.

I sigh with news that fate brought us together and I believe fate will bring us back, but for now, life is taking me on a journey.

I have been summoned by the Pennsylvania Medical Department of the Regular Army as a Major. My services will be needed mostly out in the battlefields. We surgeons are much outnumbered by wounded troops, and my life will become chaotic very quickly. I alone will not be killing but trying to save lives. I have received a field case, my "surgeon's field companion," full of instruments and that alone with knowledge will be my strength.

Don't cry, my dear. I wish that I were there to wipe your tears and take away your pain. While I dream of our life together, I feel you beside me, but then, I wake in the night with a start to this tribulation.

I have one thing to add. I couldn't hide my love for you any longer. I confessed my love for you to your father in his letter. I hope I haven't caused you difficulty, but alas, my life is in turmoil and I have to have some normalcy with it.

You see, I have asked your father for your hand in marriage, now formally, and be assured I am a man of my word, Miss Olivia Rose Bellamead. I see a smile forming on your face so I will say goodnight, but never goodbye, my true love.

My love always,

Andrew

She lay the letter down in her lap with tears falling. She realized life as she knew it was gone. How was she going to make it knowing each day and night, Andrew could be out in the mix of a battle? Her thoughts were interrupted by Benjamin approaching her.

"Olivia, I will do as Andrew asked and stay here to keep watch over you and Bella Oak."

She rose embracing her brother, so relieved that he wouldn't be leaving to join in the conflict. At least he would be safe for now. She smiled up at him holding her letter tight to her chest.

Chapter Seven

"The Hidden Room"

Instead of days moving by, months seemed to spin out of control, with only one other letter arriving from Andrew.

October Twenty-eight, 1861

My dearest, Olivia, my precious love,

The days drag on with such eeriness. I long for the day to be with you. I am presently working as a surgeon in one of the hospitals trying to piece young soldiers back together who were injured on the battlefield. So many lives of innocent men in chaos, lying before me with question after question, and I alone don't have answers for them.

I see we're more alike than we both perceived. We couldn't hide our feelings for each other, and we felt so strongly that we had to share the news of our love to your parents. I was relieved when William generously gave his permission for us to marry.

Don't fret about Jackson. Before I had seen the causalities of war, I might have been jealous of him, but now I wouldn't take away that man's only reason to survive out in the battlefields: you. I have seen and heard from the wounded about their loves at home. Love is their one saving grace that keeps them alive on all the lonely nights. Their dreams of the life they will have someday push them onward. The dream of our life together fuels me daily. It will be better for Jackson to learn of our love after he arrives safely back home.

Tell Benjamin I am so glad he has stayed to watch over Bella Oak. I, my dear, am safe for the time being and working many hours; resting few.

I do look forward to your next letter full of the tales of Bella Oak. Stay safe, my love, and don't fret so about me. I am safe at this time in a hospital. You are forever in my heart.

My love always,

Andrew

Olivia lay the letter down with the other one. She sat dreaming along with Andrew of their life together. She hoped their dream would be a realization soon.

William began to worry about the safety of his family. He called for Terrance, Jonas's son to meet with him in the office.

"Massa William," Terrance called out walking into the foyer with his hands clenched together nervously.

"Terrance, come on into the office." William stood opening the office door wide swinging his arms out welcoming in the young man.

Benjamin was sitting in his bedroom upstairs. He heard Terrance and his father talking downstairs in the foyer and raced down the stairs into the office.

"Benjamin," William spoke in a strained voice, "shut the door."

Benjamin nodded as he pulled the door shut. He turned back to his father wondering what was about to happen.

"This, my boys, is to be kept between us. Terrance, your father does know my plan. The family will soon know, including Mama Bea and James and of course, Sadie, if we can keep her quiet."

He smiled looking at Terrance. Benjamin began fidgeting and Terrance clinching his hands nervously together.

"Don't look so worried. I have decided to build a hidden room here in this office," he explained, walking around the room studying it.

"That's what this is about?" questioned Benjamin heaving a sigh of relief.

"Yes," he exhaled, "we have to have a place to hide our valuables and a safe place for the children and Ruth in case the Yankees come this way,"

"Father, have you heard more news?" Benjamin asked nervously studying his father's face, understanding his father hadn't believed the war would affect Bella Oak, but knowing the tales of battles were growing.

"No, Benjamin, jest the same news. Andrew is correct. The war is coming closer to us. That is why you are staying here to protect Bella Oak."

"Sir, I will be glad to help you," Terrance added still clinching his hands together.

"My plan is to build a new bookcase identical to this one, but move it up near the window along the side wall so no one will notice. One of the bookcases should open discreetly becoming a hidden entrance into the room."

"That will work fine," the young boy added, with his dark eyes observing William.

"It would also be nice to have another entrance in the back for an emergency escape from the house."

Terrance nodded his head taking mental notes.

"Benjamin is going to be your assistant, and he will help with whatever you require to build the room. You are the head of this project, Terrance."

Terrance grinned. He and Benjamin had been best friends their entire lives so this was going to be more of a partnership.

"You two will be able to go into town and get all of the supplies and jest tell 'em you are building Ruth some more cabinets. We have to keep this room secret or it won't work."

"Yes, Massa William, we will keep everyone safe."

"Alright, Terrance, here's some paper so you can make a list of supplies you will need," Benjamin offered. "I will get the wagon and team ready so we can head for town."

Terrance nodded his head picking up the paper. He proudly stood by William's desk and began to write.

For years, Benjamin and Terrance had studied together and Terrance had learned to read and write. They would sit down by the spring on warm days and take turns reading books to each other. Terrance, five years older than Benjamin, had grown up with many of the same advantages of Benjamin.

One of the older slaves who had done most of the woodwork inside the plantation home when it was constructed had taught Terrance to build furniture. Terrance had read and learned to become a master craftsman. He was very capable of building the new bookcases because he was so familiar with the design of the original cabinets.

Terrance grabbed his notes, hurried out the front door and down the steps of the verandah to the wagon.

William sat down at his desk peering out the window anxiously watching the young boys. He placed his elbows on his desk lacing his fingers together and exhaled nervously. This wasn't something he would have ever dreamt of building, a secret room for his family to hide in.

That afternoon the boys made it home with a wagon full of wood and supplies. They unloaded and organized the woodworking shop on the plantation.

"Olivia," called Benjamin hurrying into the home. "Yes," she called back from the parlor.

"You have a letter."

She jumped from her seat running to him. "Andrew," she called out.

"No, it's not from Andrew," he added shaking his head as he handed her the letter that had come from Georgia.

Olivia sat back down in her chair and began to read out loud. Benjamin leaned on the chair listening.

Saturday, November second, 1861

Olivia, my dear,

I hope this finds you safe. Our small militia has settled into our new lives in Georgia. We have met many soldiers from Florida along with the ones from Georgia. It's surprising how similar we all are. Most are from working farms of many different sizes, just like in our county.

The first day we arrived, they handed us our artillery. Many of the men didn't have rifles, and only a few had pistols. We also received swords, along with our uniforms. We are all now dressed in the glorious grey of the South.

I have been promoted here at Fort Pulaski to First Lieutenant under the command of Colonel Charles Olmstead. I have received my orders and I am to command the second division of Georgia and scout out some of the areas near Atlanta.

I am sending you the portraiture of me dressed in my Confederate uniform. I shall write you as many letters as possible, but unfortunately, you won't be able to send me any. I shall miss desperately hearing from you and from home.

I'm not ashamed to admit that I miss you so much and the comforts of my plantation. The weather is turning cool and I miss sitting out on the verandah watching the sunset filter through the trees. All too soon, my home will be living under the trees and keeping watch at night. My warmth will come from small campfires, not from a roaring fireplace in the comfort of my home.

A different life, indeed, but don't worry. We are a strong unit and will send those Yankees high-tailin' it back up North. They won't venture back to the South, once they've had a taste of the Confederacy.

Please pray for us, my dear, for us to come home soon. I am keeping my memories fresh of our times together and dream of our life to come. I love you, sweet Olivia, Jackson, your betrothed.

She picked up the next note and looked up at Benjamin.

Hey, Olivia,

Jackson was kind enough to allow us to send our note along with his. Tell Benjamin we have our grey Confederate uniforms and we had our portraitures made in them.

I'm sure Jackson is sending his to you. The rest of us are sending our best to you and are honored to defend The Cause.

The quarters here are cramped, damp, and cold; the food is bland: grits, hardtack, and jerky most of the time. We did have a few of the women serve us one special meal of ham, cornbread, corn and potatoes and a big piece of butter cake.

One young girl, Sylvia, who came that evening managed to catch Albert's eye. We just might be losing him to Georgia, but the rest of us are loyal to South Carolina.

We will be leaving soon, under the command of Jackson. We are hopeful that it won't be hard to take orders from him, maybe.

Olivia, Benjamin, we miss you and South Carolina so much. The days are long and the nights are filled with darkness and terror. Stories are emerging of battles getting closer.

Benjamin, please keep the home front safe so we will have something to come home to. May God keep us all protected.

Your friends, Lawrence, Jerrold, Albert, and Hansford

She placed the letter on the small table by the chair, "Those boys didn't know what they are getting themselves into. Benjamin this has to be over soon. If it drags out, it will drag the heart right out of them."

He gently patted her on the arm, "The Confederates will win and Andrew and everyone else will be home soon. I better help Terrance," he added understanding he was trying to convince himself as much as his sister.

He turned to leave, but looked back and gave his sister a reassuring look and a smile.

That fall, the sawing and hammering continued for weeks. As the bookcases began to take shape, Terrance made the oak wood as smooth as silk blending with the other wood in the office. Benjamin and Terrance worked daily as the hidden room began to take shape. The day of completion finally arrived. William stood in his office with the two young men.

"This is more amazing than I presumed it could be. No one will be able to tell this isn't jest another matching bookcase for my office."

"Thank you, Massa William," Terrance beamed so proud of his work.

"All right, you two can help me put some of Ruth's crystal, silver and other treasures inside. We also will need blankets, food, water, lanterns, a tinderbox, and anything necessary to live in there a few days. A couple of small chairs would be nice too."

"I would like a few books," Benjamin added, picking up some books from the bookcase moving them into the hidden room. "This will really protect everyone, no one will ever know about the secret room," Benjamin said proudly. "Terrance put thicker wood and rolled up old cotton and feed sacks to help keep noise down."

"We should be safe unless," William's head drooped down, "the Yankees burn her."

Olivia stood at the doorway with her eyes wide.

"Father," she shouted, "no they wouldn't do anything so horrible…would they?"

"Honey, I didn't know you were there."

"Olivia, Benjamin and I won't let nothin' happen to Bella Oak, she'll be fine," Terrance reassured.

Olivia smiled back at the boys, understanding they were so alike and both so naïve, no match for the Yankee soldiers.

"Benjamin, you can hide some weapons inside the room for me," William insisted. "Olivia will be able to fire them; however, your mother wouldn't ever touch a gun of any sort."

"You don't have to worry, Father," Olivia assured tightening her eyes with a stern look. "I will shoot anyone trying to harm us, and Joseph is a good shot, too."

"Yes, he is," Benjamin added earnestly, "I have taught him well."

"Come on, Benjamin," Olivia pulled on her brother's arm. "Let me see which pistols we can find to keep with us."

"Get my Colt Navy Revolver and some black powder and also the Remington revolver, whatever is necessary to be prepared," William called out frowning. "Don't forget the rifles."

William turned around, "Terrance," he said reaching out his hand, "thank you very much. Your workmanship is impeccable. You, my son, should never work in the fields."

"Thank you, Sir," Terrance beamed.

"When this war is over, I'm setting you up in a shop and you can start building furniture, if you would like."

"Sir," he swallowed, "that's my dream. I also, has one other request."

"Name it."

"I woulds like to marry Sadie," he said ducking his head down staring at the floor.

"Yes," Olivia announced, grabbing Terrance's arm.

"Son, you just got your answer," William laughed.

"Oh, I have to go and talk to Sadie," Olivia spun around hurrying out the room.

"Well, this will keep the women busy for a while. Congratulations, Terrance! Does Jonas know?" William questioned.

"No," he answered.

"You better go tell him soon. Olivia isn't waiting," William chuckled. "Thank you again, Terrance."

William heard the front door close as the boys stepped out onto the verandah. He leaned back in his desk chair as the soft autumn breeze from the window blew across the room. Then, he dropped his eyelids and put his hand to his forehead trying to take in the realization that life would never be the same.

Chapter Eight

"Terrance & Sadie"

Olivia and Ruth were in high spirits. Saturday, November Seventeenth had finally arrived, the day Terrance and Sadie were to wed. The thunderstorm the night before had moved on leaving clear skies and soft white clouds, a gorgeous day. At least there was some happiness at Bella Oak.

Sadie had dreamed of her wedding taking place under one of the old oaks out to the side yard. It seemed that was her special place to sit and cool off on hot summer days and she also learned she could watch Terrance from that vantage point while he worked with his father.

Sadie had been sharing a room with Mama Bea in the back of the house, but that was going to change. William decided to let the young couple live in one of the other back rooms of Bella Oak, next to James's room. He needed Terrance close if anything were to happen. Terrance puffed up with pride to be living in the grand home.

"Thank you, Sir," Terrance beamed shaking William's hand.

"Son, I trust you to help keep my family and now your family safe."

"Yes, Massa William, I won't let you down."

The winter was approaching. Wednesday, December the eighteenth arrived with a beautiful cool day. Terrance grabbed Benjamin.

"Let's go find the perfect Christmas tree," he called out, pulling him out the back door into the crisp air with Joseph running behind them.

"You wouldn't be excited about Christmas this year, would you," Benjamin hollered laughing at Terrance as the three climbed into the wagon.

A swish of the reins and the horse took off down an old path weaving through the trees deep into the woods behind the plantation home.

"Yes, siree, we shor could use some fun in that home," Terrance said pulling up on the reins.

"Miss Ruth is worn out, not herself."

"Yep, the house is too dag-burn quiet," Benjamin agreed jumping down from the wagon, "So, let's go find that special tree."

"Benjamin," yelled Joseph, "here, this is the biggest, fattest tree. Mother will love this one."

Benjamin caught up with Joseph patting him on the back.

"Yes, that's it. Come on Terrance bring the saw."

Terrance smiled at the find. He leaned down and began sawing the tree. The three loaded the large tree into the wagon and headed home.

They could hear Christmas carols coming from the parlor as Terrance pulled the wagon to a stop. He unharnessed the horse leading it to the back pasture. Benjamin and Joseph picked up the tree from the wagon carefully made their way to the back door. The door opened with Mama Bea standing there.

"Come in here! It's getting cold out there. That is a nice tree," she smiled. "Miss Ruth's going ter bes happy."

Benjamin squatted down on his knees holding the bottom of the massive tree right in front of the large window in the parlor as Terrance straighten it. Joseph set down the box full of his mother's special Christmas ornaments and decorations from the attic. He and Olivia began to decorate the huge tree just as their mother had taught them.

Annie sat to the side, singing and playing the piano. The room was coming to life, and the young people were lost in their own world, forgetting about the war for a short time.

Olivia pulled out a beautiful angel that had come from Charleston. She placed the angel on the mantel along with some holly-leaf design candlesticks and a few more trinkets of her mother's. The pungent aroma of the tree and garland made the room have the warmth of Christmas. Olivia finished decorating the room with some holly full of red berries that Terrance had cut from the side yard.

Ruth walked into the room. Silence fell over everyone. She stopped. A smile emerged as she looked at her children.

"Thank you," she proclaimed, walking over hugging each one of her children with some color coming back into her face.

She turned back around.

"Thank you Terrance," she said patting him on the back, "for your help and bringing back some happiness to this home."

"Youse welcome, Miss Ruth," Terrance answered looking around the room.

"I am so grateful to have my family safe and sound right here where they should be on Bella Oak," Ruth said beaming.

"Terrance, where's Sadie?" Ruth called out.

"She's in the back with Mama Bea."

"Tell her and Mama Bea to come here and bring James."

"Yes'am, Miss Ruth." He left the room and was quickly back, with everyone following him.

"We," Ruth announced, putting her hands up clasping them together, "may not be having our normal Christmas party however we are having our own family Christmas party. I will help make the egg nog and Mama Bea, you stir up something to eat."

"Yes' am," Mama Bea said excitedly.

"Terrance, go get Jonas and your mother. The more the merrier. We are going to have a celebration tonight," Ruth declared. "Bring back, Cyrus and Jeremiah and of course, Big John. This wouldn't be a party without him. He has the best voice and I can't wait to hear him sing."

"Yes'am," Terrance said quickly nodding his head. William heard the ruckus coming from the parlor and hurried into the room. He didn't move. He took a deep breath with tears brimming in his eyes. He had been so troubled about Ruth, but the wedding and this party was bringing her back. The strain of hearing about the war had been draining her soul and her body.

The house was alive at least for a while with everyone scurrying around preparing for the Christmas party. The food was on the dining room table along with the eggnog just as special as any party Ruth would give.

Everyone was showing up. Big John stepped into the foyer trying to wipe off his dirty clothes sending little clouds of dust down on the woolen rug. Ruth walked up next to the man standing so tall and large like an old oak.

She took his big hands in hers and kindly began, "Thank you for joining us. Please come into the parlor and have a seat."

"Thank youse, Ma'am, but's my clothes is dirty. I's better stand."

"John, we aren't worried about dirty clothes. You sit anywhere you would like."

Cyrus and Jane walked into the foyer as others followed. Ruth greeted everyone. William grabbed a few of the men, leading them into the office. He stopped and turned back around.

"Benjamin, Terrance, come on," he said waving his arm. "You two young men are old enough to have a sip of whisky. It shor will make that egg nog better," he whispered and smiled.

"It shor does, William," Cyrus chuckled patting William on the back following him into the office.

The music began to play and everyone began to sing. Then Big John stepped up by the piano. He looked at Ruth and began to sing. Everyone became quiet. His voice flowed throughout the home with calmness. Tears ran down Ruth's face, as the big black man finished the song and smiled down on the tiny woman. They each knew life was changing for them. Whether it was for the better remained to be seen. The night was amazing and it all began with one lone tree.

Christmas Day, Ruth had chicken and dressing, gravy, mashed potatoes and yams for everyone on the plantation along with freshly baked bread. The day was a day of plenty, peace, and prayer.

"William," Cyrus began standing on the verandah looking out over Bella Oak, "we have lost half of our slaves. They have left to go up North to join the Union Army."

"I understand, Cyrus," he agreed patting the man on the back. "We still have our loyal few who are going to stay awhile."

Cyrus smiled knowing many had stayed on at Bella Oak. This was their home and they weren't leaving. Many of the plantation owners were cruel, even using a whip on many, but not William. He treated his slaves fairly and kindly. This war was hard on all of them.

A letter from Andrew finally arrived the last of March.

Monday, March tenth, 1862

My dearest Olivia,

My precious love, I write with a heavy heart. I sadly have to say I shall be leaving for the battlefield in a few days. I will be under the command of Brigadier General John Parke of the Department of North Carolina, 3rd Division.

I know that I will witness the death and destruction I have only heard tales about and witnessed at the hospital. I have to admit, I am terrified of what I will encounter.

I was overjoyed to hear about your Christmas and dreamed of sitting by the tree with you in front of a warm fire, singing Christmas carols and drinking eggnog. I do like the thought of your father's eggnog.

I also loved hearing about your tales of past Christmases and can't wait until we are able to sit in front of the Christmas tree making our own memories and someday, telling them to our children and grandchildren.

How is young Benjamin doing? I understand his turning fifteen makes it harder for him to stay at home, but I do beg of him not to leave.

You talked of traveling to Charleston to visit your Aunt Violia. I plead with you to stay at Bella Oak and not venture away. I have heard rumors of Union soldiers making their way down the coast. Charleston is still in the eye of the Union and the trip could be perilous for you.

Many of the young Union soldiers are lonely needing the touch of a young woman and you, my dear, would be in jeopardy. I would be glad to accompany you to Charleston when this war is over, maybe a nice place for a honeymoon.

My father has been ill. He has worked the past few months putting in to many hours and I fear leaving him. I so wish that you were here to stay with him. Then the two most important people in my life could care for each other.

My dear, they are calling for me to leave. My love I send to you. You are in my heart as I start my new journey. Remember, my true love, this is not goodbye.

I will love you always,

Andrew

"Father!" Olivia shouted, running into his office. "Andrew is going out to the battlefields," she cried out.

William bent his head down. He too, had news of the war, "The battles…it seems are intensifying."

"He doesn't believe I should to travel to Charleston. He says it's too dangerous."

"Yes," her father added, "he may be right. I know your mother will be so disappointed, but the news is the Union soldiers are advancing into all of the Southern states." His hands tightened and wadded together, "Not good news."

The weeks passed slowly as news of battles became known. It was as the boys from home wrote in their letters: the days were long and nights came with fear.

Olivia sat up many nights peering out the bedroom window into the dark sky wondering where Andrew might be and praying he was alright.

Chapter Nine

"News"

A quiet Sunday morning, the thirteenth of April, Old Tom from the Dawson Plantation rode up on a large brown horse.

"Massa William, Massa William!" the old man shouted.

William hurried from his office. He stepped out onto the veranda with Benjamin and Olivia following.

"What is it Tom?"

"Miss Olivia," he got quiet ducking his head down.

"Go on Tom, what is it," Olivia called out to him.

He stepped up on the steps.

"We jest got news that," he took a deep breath with tears building in his old worn face, "Albert Tolleson was killed in the battle at Fort Pulaski."

"What!" yelled Olivia.

Benjamin grabbed hold of her.

"There's more…right, Tom?" William asked clinching his hands together studying the old slaves face.

"Yes Sir, Massa Lawrence has beens injured an," he stood looking over at Olivia, "Jackson Montgomery has been's captured by the Yankees."

"How bad is Lawrence injured?" William's hands gripped tighter turning his knuckles white with his body taunt.

"We don'ts knows. He's on his way home," the old man said. He stood holding onto his hat with his hands turning his hat in a circle.

"What about Jerrold Baxter and Hansford Tolleson," asked Benjamin?

"No one's knows," he answered shaking his head. "I jest bringin' word, better bes gettin' back."

"Thank you Tom. You tell everyone how sorry we are and if anyone requires my help, please let me know."

"I shor' will Massa Williams," he looked up with his tired brown eyes. "Miss Olivia, I'm sorry."

"Thank you, Tom." she said as her head bowed. Benjamin led her into the parlor.

"If they had stayed away from the fort..." Olivia cried out, "Father, why is this happening?"

"Honey, it is the way of war," he said bitterly pulling her close with his arms around her not able to take her pain from her.

She looked up into the eyes so like hers, "Andrew is in the battlefields now and I haven't heard from him."

She turned her head with tears flowing down her face. William couldn't talk. Everyone in the house was at a loss of words.

A funeral for Albert Tolleson was planned for Monday, April fourteenth. William lifted Ruth up into the carriage and Benjamin helped Olivia. Annie and Joseph sat quietly by their sides. They rode in silence down the long road into town.

The warm sun was shining through the tall trees with the scent of spring in the air. The church was packed. A few men stepped back allowing the Bellamead family to walk inside. They were led down the aisle to the front of the small church, near the Tolleson family.

Annie grabbed hold of Olivia as she looked over at Vincent. He stared back at her with his tear-stained face. He was having to say goodbye to one brother and didn't know if the other was alive. Olivia's eyes panned the crowd of people seeing Camille with her head down, knowing how worried she was for Jerrold.

Olivia felt like such a hypocrite with everyone telling her how sorry they were about Jackson being captured. This was all too much. Her friends were dying and missing and the man she loved was still out in the battlefield. Benjamin put his arm around her trying to ease her pain.

The preacher talked of the sorrow of losing such a fine young man. Sobs and sniffs were the only sound in the church. This had hit the small town of Spring Hill hard. The last prayer was for all of the young men, Albert his soul to rest, Hansford and Jerrold to be found, Jackson to be freed and Lawrence to recover from his wounds. These five young lives had an effect on the entire town. The service was ending. The congregation stood singing *Amazing Grace*.

Later that day Olivia was standing on one end of the verandah. She could hear Cyrus talking to her father and Benjamin.

"William, I talked to Edmond at the Dawson's Plantation and he told me that pour Albert's body was laid on the porch of the Tolleson's home the night before, without anyone knowing that he was there. It seems that Mrs. Tolleson was the one to find him the next morning just lying there wrapped in a worn bloody blanket. They have too many wounded," the old man shook his head. "I reckon...he was a lucky one. Most of the dead are left on the battlefield until someone can see to them for burial and many ain't making it home. They're being buried in mass graves."

She gasped. "No!" she yelled, with her voice echoing into the air. "That can't be true."

"Olivia," William shouted, running up on the verandah grabbing her.

"Miss Olivia, I'm sorry, I didn't know you were listening."

"It's alright Cyrus. She doesn't hide or run from things. She needs to know, but it is difficult to realize," Benjamin assured patting him on the back. "She'll be alright. Sometimes, I think she is the strongest of us all."

Chapter Ten
"Lawrence Dawson"

It was the morning of April twenty-ninth.

"Olivia," Benjamin screamed riding up on his horse Star Bright and waving an envelope in the air.

"Benjamin," she cried out, running to meet him, "is it?"

"Yes, it's a letter from Andrew. He is safe at least for a while."

She took the letter, sat down on the verandah, and began to read.

Thursday, March thirteenth, 1862

My dearest Olivia,

My precious love, I am now traveling on a medical train. I have left my home and will be arriving in Washington by morning. The smell of the train car is nauseating from the wounded that ride from the battlefields to the hospital. The stench of death is all around. With me, I have my belongings, my bag that was given to me that contains my canteen, blanket roll, small tent, along with paper and stamps to write home and a few other insignificant items to help me survive. This seems to be all of my worldly possessions along with my surgeon's field companion.

I am in company with a few others, not many surgeons, but a few assistants. They come from all over the North and are as lonely as I am for home and their loved ones. We each share our dreams and many tell tales of their children who they have left behind. It seems loneliness is the evil we all have to deal with for now.

The light is growing dim and I should rest. Tomorrow I will be headed South on my horse, not a train. We are to travel through Virginia to the Outer Banks of North Carolina with orders to seize the towns along the shore. It is becoming silent in this train car as each man is trying to sleep. For now my dear I say goodnight as I must sleep along with them.

My Olivia, it is another day, March the fourteenth, for me to write. Please forgive my handwriting as I am sitting with the only light and warmth of a campfire.

This morning our Unit was able to arrive in North Carolina. Our men seem eager for the battle that is to come very soon.

Major General Ambrose Burnside has given us orders to seize the towns along the inner shore. We will soon be marching to Carolina City.

We have made camp and the night air is warmer than Philadelphia, but with a crispness. The marsh has different sounds emerging from it. I have heard stories of alligators along the marsh that terrify me, whether true or not.

I will admit, it is stunning country and I wish it were under different circumstances that I am here. The reeds are standing tall with the grass swaying in the light of the moon. I fear we will have a full moon soon.

DIARY OF OLIVIA BELLAMEAD

I have always loved to sit in the peaceful night and peer up at the sky and wished for a full moon most nights, but not now. A full moon could give us away and your Confederate boys might see us. The sea is to my east, with small islands in between us and beyond is the great Atlantic Ocean.

My grandfather, who I visited when I was young, is now ailing from old age. Elderliness, I imagine as I look out at all these young lads, will not be achieved by many of them. The hush of the night is soothing and has calming effect on me, however, it is lonely. It is getting quieter as the soft whispers fade away into the night. Sleep finally comes to most. These young soldiers can be childlike when it becomes dark. They need reassuring that tomorrow will come, morning will break. Then the man inside each will emerge.

I too would love for you to be by my side at night to tell me everything will be fine and I will be safe. I also have a young boy inside of me that could use some reassuring. My Olivia, the light of the fire is growing dimmer and the silence is becoming deafening with only the soft breathing of youth. I shall need to sleep; it seems sleep is the only medicine I know to take the pain of loneliness away.

I hopefully will continue this letter soon. It makes me believe I am sitting talking to you at night, at least in my mind. That, I'm glad of! There is a fine line between sanity and insanity. My mind is a solace, helping to take my pain away, at least for now.

Don't worry, my dear, and wipe your tears for me. I am at the moment safe. Goodnight, my sweetheart, and sleep with sweet Southern dreams for us both.

My dear sweet Olivia, it is another night that I have to sit with you, but only for a few minutes. We have worked for a while, not fought any battles yet, to repair a railroad bridge.

God has blessed us and the small towns of Carolina City, Morehead City, and Newport this morning. The Union has taking them over, but the loss of life is few as the Confederates draw back.

My time is nearing that I must end this letter for now. My unit is moving in the darkness of the night to another location. We are soon to be in the mist of fighting for Fort Macon. I will continue my writing for another time. My dear, I miss you more each day and can't wait until I sit down by the spring and hear tales of you and young Benjamin.

My horse has been saddled and I regret to say it is time for me to leave. I am sending you my picture in my uniform. The uniform itself won't comfort you, but the face might.

I wish to also tell you happy birthday and hopefully I will be home soon to give you your birthday kiss. Take care my beloved; remember me in your prayers and your heart until at last I come home.

With my love always,
Andrew

She laid the letter in her lap.

"Benjamin, he is in North Carolina and the fighting hasn't been that bad. He is very lonely, but safe for now."

Benjamin stood with his lips curling into a smile.

"He will be fine, being a doctor and all," he assured nervously.

"Yes, everyone will be home soon." Her shoulders tightened as she opened the door.

"It will…all be alright," she confidently muttering to herself, still firmly gripping the letter.

The next few weeks were excruciating without news of Andrew. Olivia tried to stay busy and decided to visit Lawrence Dawson.

Benjamin pulled up on the reins of the buggy in front of the Dawson Plantation. Lawrence was sitting on his verandah.

Lawrence was the largest boy of the group from the county and also the kindest.

"Olivia, it is good to see you," he hollered out, leaning up in his chair.

His left arm was in a sling, with bandages wrapped around his body showing under his shirt. Olivia took a deep breath not only seeing his wounds, but understanding that a doctor out in the field had seen to him.

"Lawrence," she called out, as Benjamin helped her out of the buggy. "It is very good to see you."

Just like a tomboy, Olivia quickly hurried up the steps rushing over to the young boy she had known her whole life. She reached down hugging him, not worrying whether it was proper manners. He smiled up at her, never one for social graces himself. After all, they had played down at the spring each summer since they were able to walk.

"I see in your face, Benjamin, no word from the others," Lawrence suggested with worry in his eyes.

"No, Lawrence," Benjamin concluded, "I'm sure we will hear news of them soon."

Lawrence looked down at his hands, "I guess I was the lucky one of the group."

"I'm so glad you are going to be alright and everyone will be home soon. You will see; it will be fine," Olivia squatted down by her friend, who smiled back at her.

"I heard there is some news that has been circulating around the county," she brought up with a smile staring at the sweet boy in front of her.

"Yes, Mary Jane and I are getting married. We are waiting and hoping the others will be back in time."

"That is the greatest news I have heard in a long time. I will have to go into town and see her. Even amid all of this sorrow, you two will have a lovely wedding and the others would agree."

"Well…" he took a deep breath, "when I was shot lying there in the fort, all I could think about was her and the life I was going to miss. I promised myself that if I lived, I wasn't going to waste time with formalities and as soon as I was home, I asked her to marry me. Luckily, she accepted."

Olivia's mind wondered off. Lawrence observed her expression.

"Olivia Bellamead, you're not thinking about Jackson, are you? I know you too well. So, what is going on in that pretty mind of yours?" asked Lawrence.

Benjamin stood grinning.

She took in a deep breath, "I do think of Jackson, and the others, but…"

He interrupted her, "But what?"

"Remember at the picnic last summer, a young man was here from the North, Andrew."

"Yes… Now Olivia, you don't mean you have fallen in love with a Yankee?"

"Yes."

"How does he feel about all of this?"

"He loves me too and desires to come home to me, just as you wanted to come home to Mary Jane."

"Have you heard from him?"

"I have received a few letters. He is a doctor and is seeing to the wounded. He isn't fighting in the war much yet," she added.

"What a mess! However, Olivia," he assured taking her hand in his large hand, "if anyone will survive a Southerner marrying a Yankee during this war, my dear, it will be you," he added pulling her close hugging her. "I'm sorry he isn't here with you now and I will be glad to welcome him home."

"Thank you," she sniffed, wiping her eyes.

"Now sit down and tell me all about your young man and what he has had to say of the war," Lawrence directed.

Benjamin scooted over a couple of chairs and they sat and talked for the rest of the morning. All of them chatted away as they had when they were young, before the innocents of youth had been taken away.

Chapter Eleven
"John Drake"

Weeks passed and still there was no news about any missing young Rebels or Andrew. It was heart wrenching for Olivia, but she wouldn't let others see her pain. Her father was having difficulties because many slaves decided to leave and many of his once-full cotton fields were lying bare, full of dead stalks.

William planted a small field near the home with the field hands who had stayed. The worry on William's mind was growing that his dear Bella Oak would die like the young men on the battlefields.

One warm day the last day of July, Olivia was sitting trying to cool off when Terrance rode up. He jumped off his horse leaping up the stairs with a smile on his face.

"Another letter, Miss Olivia, from Mr. Andrew. I reackon he's still safe."

"Thank you, Terrance…yes," as she began to read, "he is still safe," she answered sitting back in her chair concentrating on the letter.

Wednesday, April thirty, 1862

My dearest Olivia, my precious love,

Our siege is over at Fort Macon with a small loss of life for the Union, but I dare to say, many lives were lost on the Confederates side. There were many wounded, but my assistances and I were able to see to all of the men.

My heart went out to the boys of the South. I tried to help, but my commander keeps me busy with our young men. We were ordered to care for the Union soldiers first. Regardless of how badly a Rebel soldier needed attention, he was not attended until we had done all we could do for the Union soldiers.

It was amazing how the gunfire crumbled the strong wall of the fort with our Navy bombarding from the sea. Our young men were saved by the cannons doing the job for them.

It was a sad day for me to see the white flag of surrender, but a good day to know there wouldn't be any more bloodshed. My time is nearing to leave this battlefield so I must stop for now and will continue on with my letter another day.

My sweet Olivia, I now have left the fine state of North Carolina and am sitting by a campfire writing you in the great state of Virginia, this Sunday, fourth of May. I am near the beautiful town of Williamsburg.

As of a few days ago, we are under the command of General Joseph Hooker with many other divisions arriving. This alone terrifies me. I have heard this campaign referred to as the Peninsular Campaign. The impending battle will not be small and I pray for a quick end for tomorrow's battle.

I'm sorry to be worrying you so, but I must tell someone. At least some of the men who have arrived have different food supplies. I have enjoyed a mixture of rice, peas, beans and potatoes and even some ham. Coffee is a luxury that we all drink sparingly.

My bottle of whisky I keep hidden for the wounded in case I run out of chloroform. My fellow surgeons who have arrived have warned me that supplies may not arrive on time or at all.

It is a lovely night, my dear, and I dream you are looking up at the same stars that I am and that makes me feel warm inside with a closeness of sorts.

I worry so about my father and pray he is better. I haven't heard from him, but I did receive a letter from you from the first of February.

You seemed so sad and full of apprehension. I'm dreadfully sorry that my letters have laid this burden upon you. Please remember our love is a love beyond all loves and will endure until the end of time.

I smell the saltiness in the air as the breeze is blowing from the great Atlantic. The peacefulness of the night is calming once more and so there is less movement with the massive groups all around.

I understand I should be sleeping, but I lay awake with dreams of holding you so tight. When I see you, it will be hard for me to let you go. In my dreams, I hold you each night. I know when I come home to you, I will be a stern and colder man, but my heart will melt and all of my soul will be renewed when I see your smiling face.

My dear, it has become quiet as the whispers have stopped and I regret to say I shall try and sleep. I will hold you in my dreams and sleep will eventually come. Good night, my sweetheart.

My love always,
Andrew

She looked up from the letter and Benjamin was leaning on the railing of the verandah with his eyes fixed wanting to hear news.

"He is safe, Benjamin, and has moved to Virginia from North Carolina."

"Oh, Olivia, the battles are grim in Virginia, I hear," he shrugged his shoulders with worry. "I still wish I could go help. I should become a doctor. From what Lawrence said, they can use more help. Maybe I could be an assistant."

"No, you aren't leaving too. You heard Lawrence; he doesn't want you to leave. We all need you here. Too many are gone, missing or… dead," Olivia insisted looking up at her brother.

He nodded his head agreeing.

The summer was passing with the heat intensifying. Olivia and William had sent John, Andrew's father, a letter to see how he was doing and they received distressing news back from him.

Monday, August eleventh, 1862

Dear William and my sweet Olivia,

I can't wait until I see both of you, my dear friend for life and the young girl who has captured my son's heart. My Olivia, he spoke the entire time he was here about you. Nothing else occupied that boy's mind.

I have received a few letters from Andrew, and I thank God he is safe for now. However, my fears are growing with his in the mix of battle.

I do regret to add to your misery; however, a few close medical personal and I have been infected with small-pox. Many have recovered, but I have to concede that with my immune system being low, it is a dire struggle. The fatigue is hard to overpower, but with my son out in the battlefield I have to recover and begin my work once more. There are too many depending on me to get back to the hospital.

The hospitals are overflowing with wounded in the North. This war, I suspect, isn't going well in the South.

Enough about me, I hope this finds you all well and your dear Bella Oak thriving. There is something mystical about that plantation. Andrew was captivated by the place.

He told me of her grandness with tall pines and whispering old oaks. I suppose, I too, would fall in love with her.

William, I will keep fighting to improve. We, I hope, will soon be together to sip a nice glass of scotch or some smooth Southern whisky. Take care, my friend, and may God send my son home to your sweet Olivia.

Your old and devoted friend,
John

Hearing of John's anguish, William lay the letter down on his desk, leaned back in his chair, and wiped tears from his eyes.

"He has been through enough in his lifetime: being crippled and losing his wife, now small pox. If something happens to Andrew, God help us, but especially John. I fear my friend wouldn't make it to lose his only son. That would be altogether too much sorrow."

Chapter Twelve

"Baby Benjamin"

The hot summer afternoon August the sixteenth was peaceful, but the day was scorching with steam coming from the ground after a brief shower. Olivia and Sadie were sitting on the verandah with Sadie practically smothering in the heat waiting the day for her baby to be born.

Terrance had been running around the plantation like a chicken with his head cut off nervously trying to work. William grinned watching the young man, soon to become a father, remembering those days so long ago when he too stood waiting for his children to be brought into this world.

"I don't knows, this baby is shor' taking it's time," Sadie moaned gently rubbing her stomach.

"Mama Bea said it will be soon," Olivia said tying to comfort the young girl.

"I hopes so," she declared leaning back in the rocker. "Thank yo' fur letting me jest sit's fur a while. Oh," she cried out as she leaned over looking back at Olivia with her eyes growing huge.

"Sadie, are you alright?"

"I don't knows," she cried out trying to stand from the chair.

"Terrance!" Olivia yelled.

Benjamin and Terrance raced up on the verandah and Terrance tripped over his own feet falling face down on the old plank floor at Sadie's feet.

Olivia shook her head as she smiled. Benjamin held onto Sadie's arm. After he pulled himself up off the verandah floor, Terrance held her other arm.

"Mama Bea!" Olivia yelled racing into the home following the young men as they helped Sadie on her bed in the back room.

"Alright," Mama Bea shouted, "you two go get Annella. Olivia and I can handle this," she instructed waving her arms in the air insisting that all of them leave the room.

Olivia stood in the corner of the bedroom not moving.

"If yous' gonna stay in here, yous' gonna haff to be useful," Mama Bea stated. "Go gets a pan of cool water and a rag for Sadie's brow."

Minutes ticked by with Olivia sitting next to the small bed wiping the young girl's forehead. It was hard watching Sadie every few minutes laden with pain. Sadie let out one more excruciating cry of pain, and Mama Bea reached down helping the small round baby.

Sadie fell back onto the pillow and Annella cried out, "It's a boy."

Annella lifted her grandson from the bed, gently cleaned and dressed him. The round beautiful baby cried with strong lungs. Terrance ran into the room. There lying by Sadie was his son. Sadie placed the small beautiful baby in his arms. The young man couldn't move staring down at the tiny round face baby.

"Now what do yo think Benjamin Jonas?" the new father asked, looking down on the baby boy.

Benjamin stood at the door grinning, "Let me see him."

He walked over by Terrance.

"Yes, he's a true *Benjamin*," Benjamin announced.

Terrance stood proudly with Benjamin touching the tiny baby's fingers.

"Look at his grip," Benjamin declared. "He is going to be strong. Awe he's so cute, like a little puppy."

The women looked at the two young men, one black and one white, both the best of friends who adored baby Benjamin, a new generation for Bella Oak.

The first of September brought with it a twinge of coolness only for a couple of days and a letter to Olivia, reassurance that Andrew was alive.

Tuesday, June third, 1862

My dearest Olivia, my precious love,

I come to you with a heavy heart. Forgive my penmanship as I am weary. I now understand the stories I have heard. This is hard for me to convey, and it saddens me exceedingly to write, but my dear, I must.

I have to let you and others know of the devastation that is all around. I should be resting before the next battle, but my mind won't let me. It spins out of control if I try to sleep.

This nightmare did begin as I feared, on May the fifth, 1862 with the Peninsular Campaign. The battles have continued on day and night with mangled bodies all around. I stand here with my assistants by my side, along with Chaplain Eli.

The sky is as heavy as my heart, full of dark clouds. The rain has continued with waterways overflowing their banks. It is hard to maneuver with the muddy ground being so soft, and muck has covered everyone and everything. Cleanliness is non-existent, allowing wounds to set up with infection.

The battle began with the cracks of guns and screams of men, their bodies tangled on the ground in pain. The pressure from the cannons blasting still pounds in my head. If sleep does come, these sounds are only magnified.

Some of us came upon an abandoned home, not very large, but it was dry. We set up rooms using doors as surgery tables. I laid my medical supply bag next to my work station. The soldiers would be brought in, litter after litter. My supplies were so small and the wounded so many. But, each soldier was patched with a sterile dressing to carry on their bodies as reminder always of what could be.

I worked hour after hour with myriad faces looking up at me with the same terrified look no matter what nationality, a son of the North.

My hands shook in the beginning seeing so much blood, but I soon became numb, feeling inside of each warm body repairing the damage from the round ball of the guns. My hands smelled of chloroform, as I applied it with a cloth over each frightened face.

I could hear moans of distress and men calling out to their loved ones, some believing that they actually saw family members there with them. Subconsciously knowing their destiny, the dying must have been comforted by such visions.

The chaplain was busy giving comfort when possible. I watched so many soldiers die with dignity, just as they had fought.

One young lad, Benjamin's age, was Daniel Gabriel. He laid there on the old door looking up at me with those eyes so young. I began to place the chloroform onto his face, but he reached up and stopped me first.

"Please tell my mother that I fought well and I wasn't afraid to die and for her not to grieve. I will be with my God and my fellow soldiers. I have an unfinished letter in my jacket. Please finish it and tell of good things, not sad to her. Tell how much I love her and I know I will always be in her heart."

I nodded with tears in my eyes, "Son you will be able to finish your letter, not I, and to take it home with you."

I laid the rag over his face and his young eyes closed. I began my duty of severing off his right leg, another amputation. I worked on his stomach where it had been stabbed by a sharp sword. I said a prayer for the young man, as the chaplain took him over to the side.

I continued on body after body, amputation after amputation, hoping I was at least sending the men home alive.

My body reeked with sweat and the blood of the men. I too looked wounded with my clothes red, but I only had the pain of exhaustion. I wiped my hands and ate a slice of bread that evening; I had not eaten all day and drank only a few sips of water.

The wounded didn't let up, and this left no time to rest. I worked all night with my assistant holding a lantern with a diffused light. We were so few to help so many, oh...so much suffering.

When everyone had been seen to the next day, I stepped out of my nightmare and into another. Moving outside onto the battlefield, I stood not moving. Bodies were lying in rows like cotton fields. There were soldiers I didn't even have a chance to save, Northern and Southern alike each with their bloody uniforms, not caring whether they were blue or grey.

With a light drizzle floating down upon them, the dew became their swathe. I stepped among the dead men with many of their eyes still looking up to the sky. The fog was softly lying out in the valleys with serenity, and I prayed for God and his angels to minister to the grieving and wounded. I believe the misty rain acted as God's tears for lives that were cut away too short. The pain I felt will never leave my mind.

As I stepped back into the home, I saw Chaplain Eli leaning over Daniel Gabriel with a solemn face. He lifted up the young boy's jacket and pulled out a wrinkled letter that Daniel had scribbled.

Chaplain Eli turned around as I walked up, "Andrew, the address is on the letter. From the words in the letter the young boy didn't believe he would make it through the battle. He was a brave lad."

I shook my head as my voice wouldn't work, my throat choking me. I sat down in the dim light of the lantern and told a mother of her brave son, of how he died with dignity, and of his heroism for his country. I told her not to mourn, that wasn't what he wanted. He wanted her to be proud of him and remember him as a brave soldier doing his duty for his country and fellow soldiers. My soul was overcome with grief as I wrote of his last words.

My heart broke as a doctor. I knew with adequate surgical equipment and sterile surrounding this young lad that he would have outlived his mother and grown old.

My dear, the battles continued on for the entire month of May. This campaign is commonly called Bloody May.

I believed I had seen the worst of the war, but I was deceiving myself. Our band of soldiers arrived in Fair Oaks Station, Virginia and the battles began with more and more troops of both sides arriving.

My body ached with excruciating pain as I had stood the month of May cutting on men one after another. One time, I'd had all I could take, and I left the confinement of the makeshift hospital and went out onto the battlefield. I stood among the men, young and old, as they fell with a thud to my feet. The roar of the cannons and gunfire echoed in my head along with cries of pain and terror from the Union and the Johnny Rebels falling to the wet ground. Each cried out for assistance as I leaned down not worried which side they had come from. So many moaned taking their last breath as they lay still with their eyes looking up at me. I reached down closing their serene eyes. Peace would come over them at the end.

My body shook with a strong desire to yell stop, no more, cease! Seeing the red puddles, I blinked as I fell to the ground on top of some of the soldiers feeling their warm dead bodies beneath me. I felt the pain in my side as I looked down seeing red running warm from my body. I had been shot.

I now was lying there among the dead. My thoughts were as the others who I had known were dying: wanting to call out to loved ones, wanting to see loved ones standing near me, understanding Daniel Gabriel's fear that his loved ones would suffer because of my death.

I reached down pressing my wound with my hand letting the blood trickle through my fingers. I stood with blood flowing down my leg, joining the blood of the others. The will to live drove me as I pushed myself back to the makeshift hospital.

Chaplain Eli saw me and grabbed me. My mind went blank as the cloth came over my face and when I awoke, there was a bandage on my side. I was one of the lucky ones.

I came to understand the pain and fear of the men as I stood with dizziness. Chaplain Eli tried to get me to lie back down back on the hard floor, but I had an obligation, I thought. However, the surgeon who had operated on me ordered me down for the next twelve hours.

"You're too hazy and weak to help, and if you exert yourself now, you could start to bleed, so rest, my good man. I outrank you. Rest, that is an order," the doctor hollered.

Later, I continued on with the barrage of men on stretchers, until the wounded, now thousands in one month, were seen to. I took more time to show mercy and speak a kind word to ease their suffering, understanding the fear they were living with.

This battle did come to an end as I sat down pulling out my bottle of whisky taking a sip and passing it around to the surgeons and assistances, even Chaplain Eli. Our celebration time was ended after only a few minutes because work to prepare the men to leave our hospital to board trains to go genuine hospitals in the North was posted and ordered.

I sighed knowing that many wouldn't make it back because disease was winning the battle. Many would die from infections of blood poison and gangrene. Such a waste! I squeezed my hands together tightly turning my knuckles white. I could have saved so many more with sterile conditions. But there are no such conditions on a battlefield.

To my great surprise, I have been ordered to board the train home to recuperate. I sit here in one of the same cars that I arrived in. I am remembering the sounds at night between each battle like the voices of the soldiers singing way out over the valleys. Many, my dear, were your rebels.

One such song stayed with me, "I am a Rebel soldier and far from my home, I am a Rebel soldier and far from my home." The words keep flowing in my mind. I can still hear the beating of the drums of both sides and with the eerie beat stopping in the quietness, so do many heart beats.

My Olivia, I am tired but very much alive. I will write you from my home, as I will be traveling home to stay with Father, a small pleasure in all of this devastation. Good night, my sweetheart, and once more sweet Southern dreams.

My love always,

Andrew

"Father," she screamed, "Andrew has been shot!"

Benjamin and William ran into the room. She handed them the letter. William began the tales of war as she sat there with a blood-drained face.

"But, Olivia, he is alive and well. Since he will be at his father's, you can quickly write him a letter back," William swallowed.

"No, Benjamin," she said, without his saying a word in response. "Please," she stood not saying anything else as she made her way up the stairs to her room. She couldn't have him leave her, not now.

Chapter Thirteen

"Homecoming"

Months passed. Olivia received letters from Andrew with reassurance that he was still safe for the time being. He wasn't departing for the battlefields for a while, even though his wound had healed.

His father needed assistance and he wasn't leaving him until he was stronger. She felt like her heart would stop when a new letter arrived, fearing that Andrew was back on the battlefield.

The first of December, Benjamin came running into the home and office out of breath, yelling, "Father!"

"Benjamin," William leaped from his chair terrified. "What is it boy?"

"No, nothing's wrong!" he quickly shouted, "This is a grand day."

Olivia and Ruth stood at the office door holding onto each other.

"Spit it out son; don't keep us guessing!" William called out scooting around his desk. "Jerrold, Hansford, and Jackson are home."

Olivia ran to him screaming, "Are they alright?"

"Jackson is drained and malnourished, but he will be fine. He said he'd had lice while he was imprisoned, but that he got that remedied as soon as he got on Southern soil. Jerrold received a wound in his leg, but the doctors said he wouldn't lose it. And, Hansford was shot in the arm, but is healing up."

"When can we see them?" questioned Olivia.

"Soon, but Olivia…" Benjamin began, "you are going to have to tell Jackson the truth about your engagement. That isn't going to be easy.

"I know, but I am so, so happy they are alive and back home."

"Where have they been?" asked William wrapping his arm around Ruth and taking in a deep breath of relief.

"It seems Hansford and Jerrold followed the Union soldiers with their captured Rebels and waited until they had the opportunity to free them. They risked their lives to save many and are now heroes."

"That's my boys," Olivia said so proudly. "Mother, we should have a celebration, a small one here at Bella Oak for the heroes who are home. Bella Oak can have its Christmas party this year."

"Yes," Ruth grinned squeezing William. "I will go and tell Sadie to start preparing and Benjamin, you find out for me when the boys will be able to come over."

"Mother," Olivia said solemnly, "in the morning, I'm going to visit Jackson."

"Yes, dear, I think you should," she offered, patting her daughter's arm. She spun around hurrying out into the foyer.

"Will you go with me, Benjamin? I don't think I should go alone," Olivia added nervously.

"Sure," Benjamin nodded his head yes. "I agree the sooner the better. Are you ready for this?"

"After what Jackson has been through, I think he will understand how life changes. I do care for him and it is so hard to think about hurting him."

"Yes, but in time, he will be fine. We will leave first thing in the morning," Benjamin agreed.

"Mother," Olivia called out, going to the back of the house, "I will have to invite Etta. I know she will be thrilled to help Jackson return to some semblance of normal."

"Well, sweetie, you and Benjamin can write down some names and I will add mine to the list," Ruth replied, beginning her own notes.

Olivia stopped in the foyer. She looked up the long staircase and then stepped slowly up the stairs with her thoughts swirling. The sun was shining into her bedroom. She picked up her stack of letters from Andrew along with his picture and got comfortable on her window seat. She leaned back against the window frame and quietly began to read the first to the last letters she had received. Looking at Andrew's picture and remembering the passion she felt with him holding her, she reached up touching the necklace he had given her, their love a love beyond all loves.

Jackson was a friend and would always be a friend. She didn't want to lose their friendship, but Andrew was her one true love and nothing would ever change her mind. She could see the old oak sitting way upon its hill remembering the dance music flowing with Andrew's arms wrapped tightly around her, lost in their own time.

The next morning came too soon. She finished her breakfast and straightened her dress and hair. It was time to leave. Benjamin brought the buggy around. Knowing her mission, Terrance helped her into the buggy. He gave her a grin of encouragement and nodded an affirmative *yes* to her.

The morning was chilly with a breeze blowing as they made their way down the road. Listening to the wheels of the buggy crunching the rocks underneath them, they approached Jackson's home. Wanting to stir up as little road dust as possible, Benjamin pulled up on the reins and the horse slowed down.

There standing sturdy were the gates of the Montgomery Plantation. Olivia shuddered and pulled her wrap up around her neck. She was trying to prepare herself as thoughts were spinning in her mind as to what she had to say. She took a deep breath.

There in front of them was the huge plantation home with old Tom standing out front with a smile on his face. Benjamin pulled up on the reins and the horse stopped. Tom stepped up helping Olivia out of the buggy.

"Miss Olivia and Mr. Benjamin, it shor' has been a while. How's yo' family been doing?"

"Doing fine, Tom. How's Jackson feeling?"

"He was feeling poorly when he gots home, but is better now. Yor visit will helps him, Miss Olivia."

"Thank you, Tom. It's nice to see you," she answered kindly, with a guarded look growing on her face.

Benjamin leaned over slipping his arm around hers.

"Remember, Andrew. Olivia, you have to do the right thing."

Her head nodded. She pulled her shoulders straight as a true Southern woman would do.

Tom opened the door and stepped back. "Miss Olivia, Mr. Benjamin, please come in."

Benjamin and Olivia stepped into the huge foyer. The aroma of fresh baked bread drifted throughout the huge home.

Zachariah stepped up. "Well, I wondered how long it would take you to come welcome Jackson home. My dear, how are you doing?" he questioned Olivia as he took her hand in his.

"A lot better now that our boys are home and safe."

"Benjamin, it's a pleasure to have you two here," he answered shaking Benjamin's hand. "Jackson is in the parlor."

Benjamin and Olivia followed Zachariah into the large room. Olivia gasp as she saw Jackson sitting covered with a small throw in an overstuffed chair by the crackling warm fire.

Jackson was thin and his face was colorless, drawn, and tight. He looked feeble and frail, not the strapping young man before. But, he had a big smile on his face. He reached out his arm.

"My dear sweetheart, come near. I apologize, but I jest don't have the energy to stand."

"That is understandable, Jackson, I'm jest so glad you're safe and home," she whispered squatting down next to him. He pulled her close and kissed her cheek.

"My dear, your hands are like ice. Come near the fire and warm yourself," he said looking up.

"Benjamin, it is nice to see you again," Jackson assured reaching out his hand to shake. "Thank you for staying here and keeping Olivia safe. Now sit and tell me how things are going."

"Jackson," she asked feeling overwhelmed, "I would like to talk to you in private for a few minutes, if that is alright?"

"Of course, my dear," he replied. "Don't look so strained. I am going to be fine. I jest require some good home cooking and rest for a while."

Benjamin and Zachariah left the room and closed the door. Olivia scooted an ottoman next to Jackson. Tears grew in her eyes and dropped slowly off her cheeks. Jackson started to speak, but she stopped him.

"Jackson, this is so hard for me, but I have to jest begin. Please," she sniffed, "I don't want to lose your friendship, but I have to break off our engagement. I care so much for you and didn't want to hurt you," she added ducking her head with tears falling onto his blanket.

He took a deep breath, and lifted her head so he could look into her eyes. A smile came on his face.

"I see, my dear Olivia, I have heard from Lawrence the news. He hoped to ease our pain, so this wouldn't be so difficult on you or me or bad timing with everyone around. I knew at the picnic I was losing you. I could feel you pulling away from me. I now understand it was that Yankee. It is difficult on me to think that you have fallen in love with one after the treatment I have received, but my dear, I must let bygones be bygones."

"You don't hate me?"

"I could never hate you, Olivia. I have loved you since I was young, but your heart was captured by someone else, and that I must live with."

She leaned over putting her arms around him resting her head on his chest sobbing.

He patted her back as he pushed her hair back from her face. Now bring young Benjamin in and tell me what has been happening while I have been away."

She looked at him and smiled. She wiped her face and called for Benjamin to come back into the room. He looked at her and she nodded her head that everything was fine.

"Now," Benjamin began, "Mother would like to have a celebration soon when you are feeling better.

"Oh, my mother will be thrilled. This war is wearing her down," Jackson added straighten up his throw and getting his composure back.

"Yes, I can imagine, but this is going to be a fun celebration." She stopped talking and squeezed her mouth together briefly, then said, "except for Albert...."

"Yes," Jackson began, "but he wouldn't like us to sit around and mourn him. He had too much life. I was with him when he died and he talked for a few minutes before he drew his last breath. I couldn't help him. I felt so horrible not able to help as I held him in my arms. He wasn't in pain. He talked calm, wanting me to tell everyone how much he loved all of you and was worried about his family grieving so. He told me he was going to be all right and was more worried about Hansford and the rest of us. He looked up at me, exhaled a sigh, and fell back in my arms. I laid him on the ground and tried to get my composure back when I saw Lawrence get shot and fall to the ground. It was horrifying thinking he was dead too. I didn't learn he was alive until they came to save me."

"I'm so sorry you had to go through that," Olivia assured, remembering Andrews's accounts of the wounded and the one young boy dying, only worrying about his mother.

"Well, I'm home now and it is time for a celebration. I will speak with the others and we will set a date."

They continued talking as he told tails of camping out, traveling to Atlanta, and meeting so many young men from different parts of the South.

Chapter Fourteen
"Christmas Dreams"

It was December fourteenth and Olivia and her mother were preparing for the Christmas celebration. Mama Bea had sent Benjamin and Terrance into town for supplies, hoping there would be some, as the general store was becoming bare.

The women were still able to make their fried pies from dried apples from last summer; they only had to have flour and sugar. They had cooked a huge hog and had some sweet potatoes from the cellar. There would be enough food for the party. All still believing the war would be over soon. It seemed to help the women now that the boys were home and were well. Not seeing or hearing the real story was a blessing in disguise.

Olivia heard the wagon pull up and she rushed out the front door to help. Benjamin and Terrance had bought more supplies on her behalf. They knew things weren't getting better after their talk with Jackson. Benjamin jumped down from the wagon seat.

"Olivia," he hollered, "another letter from Andrew."

She took the letter in her hands holding it up next to her heart.

"Go on and read it. We can unload and store the supplies; we know where to put them," Benjamin insisted.

Terrance grinned.

She hurried to her room and became comfortable on her window seat.

Monday, December First, 1862

My dearest Olivia, my precious love,

I first would like to wish you a very Merry Christmas. I dare say, it is nice to be home for Christmas and my Christmas wish and present would be you. I had hoped the war would have ended by now and we would be together, but alas, I will have to wait until next year to spend Christmas with you. Then, I will be able to sit by the warm fire close to you.

My days are long and my nights are lonesome. I leave before dawn and arrive home late in the night. The weather is cold and rainy with a chance of snow.

I feel anguish for the young lads out in the battlefields. As a youth, I couldn't wait until the first snow of the season, preparing for the cold with my sock hat and gloves, but now I dread thinking of the bodies freezing out in the small tents that only hold back some of the wind.

It saddens me so knowing the solitude that the boys are feeling in their hearts being away from their loved ones on Christmas. I'm sorry I am sounding so dreadful, but I feel guilty sitting here in my warm room after eating a nice meal.

I do recognize my work of repairing and sending home these lads, but looking into their sad and still terrified eyes and understanding their fear is so hard for me. Their lives have changed with their innocence vanishing and I comprehend what they must live through in their minds the rest of their lives. I don't know whether they are lucky or unlucky.

Many women have volunteered to help see to the men and have been bringing food and papers to help many write home. It seems a small comfort to the men hoping to be home soon. There is some brightness in all the gloom. Many we are sending home will be able to make it there by Christmas day, a present that they and their love ones will never forget.

I can't wait until I receive your letter telling me of your Christmas at Bella Oak. With young Benjamin around, there is never a dull moment. Please tell him happy birthday for me. Sixteen, it will be harder to keep him from the battles. I pray the war will end soon and he will not have to participate in it.

We aren't decorating a tree this year or putting up any garland. There just isn't any time, but I do see some decorations as I ride to work and many of the volunteers have begun to sing Christmas carols to cheer up the men.

Memories of Christmases of long ago and dreams of my future pass through my mind as I picture a Christmas tree with candles and a fireplace flickering with warmth and light. I will be sitting playing music and you, my dear, rocking our child in the comfort of Bella Oak. These dreams still keep me sane as each night passes.

The time is now two o'clock and I must be leaving by four, so I must rest with these warm thoughts in my mind. Goodnight, my love and Merry Christmas.

My Love Always,

Andrew

She couldn't move with tears dropping down onto the paper, but all the tears weren't of sadness, most were about the hopes and dreams of the future. With baby Benjamin around, the future was much brighter and her dream she hoped more of a reality.

She sat there in the quietness for the moment saying a prayer for all the ones out in the battlefields, Union and Rebels, then a soft prayer thanking God that Andrew was safe and warm. That was the best Christmas present for her this year.

She laid the letter on top of the others, knowing there was much to be done. As she stepped down the stairs, she could hear Benjamin and Terrance laughing while decorating another Christmas tree. Her mother and Mama Bee and the others were bustling in the kitchen. Her father was busy in his office. The boys were home. Yes, there was much to be thankful for.

Chapter Fifteen
"The Christmas Party"

It was the afternoon of December the eighteenth and the celebration was about to begin. Everyone was ready as Bella Oak lit up with warmth coming from the ole gal if only for a few hours. Carriages began to arrive and the Montgomery's were the first.

Jackson was more like himself physically, but not mentally. The war had changed him. He wasn't solely concentrating on his plantation anymore. He had a lot of additional things now on his mind.

He leaned in and Olivia grabbed him throwing her arms around his neck. He kissed her on the cheek, a sign that proper social etiquette was gone. The younger bunch wasn't worrying about what their mothers thought.

The Dawson's arrived next. Olivia grabbed Lawrence as well. The huge young man lifted her off the floor with a hug, swirling her around in a circle. She kissed him on the cheek as he smiled down on her.

The next was the Baxter family. She ran out to the verandah not letting Jerrold get to the front door. Again her arms extended, Olivia grasped the hands of the young man and she pulled him close to her.

"I'm so glad you're home and I know that Camille is too," she said smiling up at Jerrold's hazel eyes.

"Yes, she is. Now, I believe she is to be here tonight," he answered with a grin on his face, knowing all too well that she would be.

"She wouldn't miss this for anything. Come inside. It is freezing out here," she added as he took her arm.

She could see his body limping to the door, the doctor had saved his leg, but he would always have a reminder of this war. Benjamin reached over to him and the two young men hugged each other.

Olivia looked around. Walking up to the verandah was the Tolleson family. Tears were building dropping down her face seeing only Hansford, but not Albert. Albert was like Benjamin, so full of life and at every picnic and party. He and Benjamin would make a stir. Hansford saw her with tears in her eyes and swallowed hard trying to choke back his own tears.

"Olivia, Albert wouldn't like you to be tearful. You know he'd be causing a stir to take your mind off the sadness. Let's make this day happy, if not for ourselves, for Albert."

"I miss him and I have missed you, my old friend," she added with her arms around his neck.

She wasn't worried that he came from a small farm on the other side of town. He was her friend.

She saw Vincent standing behind his parents. Olivia had invited him to this party so he didn't have to sneak around to see Annie.

Annie was standing over to the side waiting and watching for Vincent. She knew in a few years her mother wouldn't have a choice and she would marry Vincent. Olivia could see the determination in her sister's eyes.

Many others started to spill in to Bella Oak. Camille came in, her face beaming. She grinned at Olivia as she hurried over to Jerrold. Etta stood staring at Olivia trying to figure out why she would break off her engagement to Jackson. As their eyes met, Olivia smiled at Etta and her face lit up with a smile as well.

The food was just as always so delicious and the men ended up in the office, along with Benjamin and Terrance sipping whisky.

Annie started playing Christmas carols and the small group began to sing. A few of the men became more boisterous as the whisky helped them sing a little louder than normal. The cheers and laughter along with the music was flowing from the huge plantation home.

Ruth walked in holding onto Big John's massive arm. He was dressed in clean nice clothes. The large room became quiet. Everyone gasp when she led him to the piano.

"It is my pleasure to present our beloved John, and he is going to perform for us a few of my favorite Christmas carols."

William watched his tiny wife standing by the large back man, not worrying anymore about protocol or social graces.

The music began to play and John's voice rang out with everyone standing quietly with smiles emerging. His voice once more was as if it was coming from an angel. The familiarity of the songs filling the home took the cares and hardships of war away.

His voice became quiet and everyone cheered, but then Hansford stepped up to the huge man, "Sir, I have a request, if you don't mind?"

Big John stood staring down at the young man who had called him *Sir*, "Mista Hansford, anything, anything yous'd like."

"My brother, Albert loved to sing and he sang one song over and over that his voice repeats in my mind," he paused for a second, trying to get his composure back.

"What song, Mista Hansford."

"*I am a Rebel Soldier and Far From my Home*, do you know that song?"

"Yes Sir," the large man answered looking over at Annie as she shook her head no.

"That's alright," he said as he took in a deep breath looking out at the young Rebels from the county standing before him. His strong deep voice didn't require accompaniment of a piano.

> *"Oh, Polly! Oh, Polly! It's for your sake alone,*
> *I left my dear old father, my country and my home,*
> *I left my dear old mother to weep and to mourn,*
> *I am a Rebel Soldier and far from my home."*

The words kept flowing and Olivia stood by the fireplace with tears running down her face remembering Andrew telling her of listening to the song out on the battlefields at night coming from the young Rebels. She could see Albert sitting by the campfire all alone singing the sad song.

The words continued, *I am a Rebel Soldier and far from my home*! Once more the lyrics continued, *I am a Rebel Soldier and far from my home*! And then it was quiet. Everyone stood not moving or talking as Hansford shook Big John's hand. The big man didn't move as the young rebels of war walked up and took turns shaking the man's hand for his singing ability, not for glorifying the war. Nearly all of them and Big John stood in humility, and the cause for the war seemed a distant memory.

Ruth didn't want the Christmas party to end on such a low note, "Why don't we play *Packing the Trunk*?"

The men arranged the chairs in a big circle. The participants sat down.

"Come to the middle with me, Big John. You're going to be the spinner," declared William.

William and Big John went inside the circle. Big John got blindfolded with William's handkerchief.

"Alright, John, I'm going to turn you around a couple of times and then you point at someone to take a turn," explained William.

Etta was chosen first, so she had to pretend that she was going on a trip and had to pack something in the trunk that started with an *A*.

"I believe I'll pack an Ace in case I need to have one up my sleeve!" Etta exclaimed, making the group giggle to think of a Southern lady gambling in a saloon.

"Good one, Miss Etta. Who will be next? That is the question. Are you ready to spin again, John?"

"I recon so," answered John as he put his blindfold back in place.

The next to be chosen was Camille, who was tasked with putting something in the trunk that began with a *B*. She hesitated for a minute seeming to have gone blank.

"A brush, a brush for my hair," she exploded.

And so, the game went until the night was almost spent. People began to leave and Olivia wished everyone a Merry Christmas and a Happy New Year.

"I hope the New Year brings us an end to this war and peace to our plantations," Olivia said as she waived goodnight to the Montgomeries and the Tollesons, who were the last guests to leave.

That night, Olivia lay in her bed with the eerie words of *I Am a Rebel Soldier* repeating in her head. She tried to get a Christmas carol in her mind, but that war song was stuck there until sleep overcame her.

Chapter Sixteen
"Yankees on Bella Oak"

The New Year, 1863 came in at Bella Oak with an austere quietness as the war continuing in years now, not months. Olivia sent Andrew many letters since he was home. She wrote him nightly and would send a group of letters at a time.

"Olivia, another letter from Andrew," Benjamin hollered one cold March day as he leaped up on the verandah, hurrying into the home.

She ran to the door gratefully clutching the letter he gave her. She raced up the stairs with her skirt pulled high as not to trip. Olivia settled into her spot by the window, carefully tearing open the envelope.

Sunday, February the eight, 1863

My dearest Olivia, my precious love,

I have much enjoyed your daily letters telling me of your life at Bella Oak, that I am sorry to say, I will miss. My time at home with

Father has come to an end. I have been transferred, no my dear, not directly on the battlefield, but close to a centralized field hospital. I am under the command of General Amiel Whipple of the third division III Corps. He seems to be a fair man, a surveyor, an engineer, a military man, but not one experienced with infantry. He too doesn't belong on the battlefield.

This, I'm afraid, is a similar unit to the one I was in before, but these hospitals are in larger homes or buildings and more medical supplies available, along with the luxury of more intense surgery. The wounded are treated in the hospitals and then taken to tents with cots, where doctor assistants see to them. This system is by far more humane than the one on the battlefield where wounded soldiers lay on the hard ground with only a blanket if possible.

But alas, I will be out of touch for some time. I will write as often as possible. Battles are intensifying and the number of wounded is growing. I fear seeing the wounded coming at me without an end. I once more, am not ashamed to say that I am afraid, not for myself but for you. If something should happen to me, you are too young to bury yourself in grief.

I again have my bag ready along with my surgeon's field companion prepared. I will leave at daylight on that horrible medical train. I will send you as many letters as possible so you won't worry so.

My dear, it is getting late and my eyes are tired. Yet again, I must say goodnight and may your Southern dreams be filled with our love.

My love always,
Andrew

She sat there crying. It had helped her so to be able to write to him each night. She squinted, her eyes.

"Olivia Rose, stop your pouting," she shamed herself. "You are safe; it is Andrew who will be in danger."

She comforted herself by deciding to keep writing each night. Then when he came home, she would present him with his stack of letters. They would be able to talk for days about all he had missed at Bella Oak. Reading her letters would be a way for him to catch up about the pertinent news of the county.

Peering out into the afternoon, she sat there feeling the cold from the frosted window. She began to see snowflakes falling. They were so soft and pure falling from the heavens. For her this was calming, but short-lived when she thought about so many soldiers being out in the cold and wet.

Olivia shook her head trying to get that thought out of her mind. For now, she should enjoy the snowfall. She smiled to herself knowing Benjamin and Terrance would be out playing like little boys. It would not be long before Little Benjamin would be out joining them in snowball fights.

The cold winter was unrelenting and the end of March was approaching. William sat down at the dining table at supper and looked out over his children. Ruth dropped her head and sniffed.

"My dear sons and daughters, I have news. I have been called to Charleston for business. Being a lawyer, I have been requested to assist some of the men. I will be staying there for a few weeks and I hope, not longer."

"Father, I shall go with you," Benjamin quickly spoke with excitement in his voice.

"No, son, you are staying here to watch over the plantation. You will be in charge of this great place. It is a lot of responsibility for you."

Benjamin ducked his head understanding, but still wishing he could leave.

"Your mother, too, would love to join me on my trip, but the word is grim in Charleston and I fear for her safety, so she shall stay here."

"We will be fine, Father," Olivia spoke up, looking into her father's sad eyes.

"Yes, Father, don't worry. We can handle Bella Oak for a few weeks," Joseph responded trying to act grown up.

"That I am assured of. My children are strong and so is Bella Oak."

"When do you leave?" asked Olivia.

"In the morning, I regret to say," William added overwhelmed as he stood. "I will say my goodbyes tomorrow."

"No, Father. As Andrew says, we will never say goodbye, but goodnight," Olivia assured smiling back at her father's heartrending expression.

"Yes, my dear. I will be back soon, so this won't be goodbye," he said leaning over with his hands on her shoulder. Ruth stood and he reached his hand out to her, and then the couple slowly retreated from the dining table and walked up the stairs together.

"Oh, I still wish I could go with Father," Benjamin declared firmly gripping onto the back of his chair.

"No, you can't leave us. There is a lot for you to see to here, Benjamin," Olivia asserted. "I overheard father talking to Cyrus about the Yankees and there are small groups of them hiding out on some of the plantations along the river, out in the back fields. This war is spilling over into our private lives. It makes me sick to think of battles being so close."

"Yankees on Bella Oak! I will do some checking tomorrow after Father departs," Benjamin injected. "Now, don't look so worried, I will be careful. I will be on a hunt and they will be the hunted."

"Well, you do know the lay of the land better than they do, but you stay out of their sight. They are trained military men and you are only a hunter," Olivia said anxiously. "But, you and I can handle those damn Yankees. I'm sure of it!" she exclaimed trying to sound more supportive.

Benjamin grinned back at his sister, a true spitfire.

The next morning was difficult as they stood hugging their father, each child telling him how much they loved him. All prim and proper like a Southern lady, Ruth stood without tears falling, but her face was drawn tightly and her eyes had not had any sleep.

William prepared to leave. Benjamin held onto his mother standing along with the other children on the verandah.

Big John rode up. "Sir, I's a'going wit youse."

"Oh, John, I don't know, it may be dangerous. You are a free man, and you don't have to go with me."

"Well Sir, if I's be a free man, then I is a'going wit youse," he said smiling, looking over at Ruth. "Miss Ruth, I's will bring him back to youse."

"Thank you, John. I hope you both come back real soon," she added smiling back at the huge man.

William stepped off the verandah lifting his boot up into the stirrup and swinging up onto the saddle. He looked young sitting on his horse so straight and tall. He grabbed the reins and turned back.

"I won't say goodbye, my family. I will be home soon," he assured turning to leave. He stopped down by the line of old oaks looking back at the plantation home, waving.

Ruth turned back to the door without saying a word. She lifted her dress so ladylike stepping up the stairs. Olivia knew there was so much sadness around the small town with so many loved ones gone from home. So many men had been killed and brought home for burial leaving wives and mothers with another onerous responsibility, to see to many farms.

Benjamin did as he said going on his hunting trip. He came home late that evening with news.

"Olivia, Terrance, please, join me," he whispered, rushing into the office and over to the fireplace in front of the leather office chairs.

They turned following him into the office.

Benjamin stood and rubbed the palms of his hands in front of the fire.

"Benjamin," Terrance voice rose, "what is the news?"

He turned to face the two.

"It was like Cyrus and father said. I spotted a group of about twenty Union soldiers down by the river. I spied on them listening. It seems there are more along the river. They are using the water way to travel."

"You and I should go take 'em," Terrance suggested, making fists.

"No, we aren't a match for them and there are too many," Benjamin protested. "But, I am going back each evening and listen to their plans. They do talk a lot at night, I guess to pass the time."

"Oh, this isn't good if they're…that close," Olivia added. "The hidden room should have everything available and furnished with what we might need for a while. Terrance, Sadie needs to put some of Baby Benjamin's things inside."

"You also should keep your pistol with you at all times," Benjamin moaned. "I will get Joseph to strap on his gun. Terrance you will have to tell Jonas that he should carry his. I will talk to Cyrus, too."

"What were the men like?" questioned Olivia with thoughts of Andrew being a Union soldier.

"The truth?" Benjamin asked."

"Yes,"

"They were tired, uniforms worn, many were talking of going home knowing they should be getting ready to plant their crops for the spring. One man was talking about his children, how he hadn't seen them since the war began, understanding how much they had grown and changed. Some were talking about holding their wives and sweethearts. I could see the fear and loneliness in their faces just as Jerrold and the boys talked about, and you've read Andrew's letters stating the same information."

She sat there in front of the warm fire in the leather chair staring off thinking of Andrew.

"It's difficult, at one point I had a longing to shoot each of them, but then I picture Andrew in my mind, sitting there by the fire writing you. There were a few that aren't decent men. They have a mean streak in them a mile wide."

"How do you know that, Benjamin?" Olivia asked.

"By what they said they intended to do to people around here."

"What did they say?" fired off Olivia.

I...I don't like talking about this with you, but I know you'll keep insisting until you get details," Benjamin took a deep breath. "They sit around bragging about what they intend to do to the Rebels and their women. They are planning on more than battlefield fighting; they intend to pillage and loot every plantation home in the county."

"This war!" Olivia exclaimed. "When will it ever be over? I just want everyone to go home."

"I understand, but Olivia, if those men come this way, you can't hesitate to shoot. Don't think about Andrew being one because he's not. They are brutal soldiers and will kill us and burn Bella Oak over our heads if they get the chance."

"I won't let those Yankees harm us or Bella Oak. I know the difference, Benjamin," she assured, "but it won't make it any easier."

Terrance was leaning by the door, "I will get Sadie prepared and then tell my father. I'll get my pistol and have it handy too," he said shaking his head turning to leave.

"Thank you, Terrance, for staying here." Benjamin assured patting him on the back, "You are a free man now."

"I've always been free," he said smiling, "This is my home too, my Bella Oak."

Benjamin smiled at Terrance, but as Terrance left, the smile faded. The carefree innocence of youth was disappearing from Benjamin's face.

"How is mother doing?" Benjamin questioned with uneasy green eyes and frown lines showing.

"She won't come out of her room. She eats and stays right there. I'm really concerned. She wasn't raised to deal with anything like this. We can't worry her with this news of the Yankees. I guess, we are like Father, real Bellameads."

"Yes," Benjamin grinned putting his warm hand on her shoulder, "we will be fine. Let's not worry, but stay focused. Remember, those Yankees are the ones to be worried," he assured.

Chapter Seventeen
"Charleston"

The next few weeks, everyone was on lookout. The children hadn't been raised to stand guard with their guns by their side ready to shot if the Yankees came near, but Olivia and Benjamin weren't letting their father down. Annie was too timid to carry a gun, so like their mother. Although Sadie had been like Annie, She was strong now. She was like a mother bear with a cub.

Many slaves had left. The once vibrant plantation was bare and so quiet. But, a few slaves had stayed because they felt at home at Bella Oak, and they would defend it as if it were their home if need be.

Another letter arrived from Andrew. Olivia held it in her hands seeing his writing on the envelope.

"He's still safe," she whispered.

Wednesday, March twenty fifth, 1863

My dearest Olivia, my precious love,

It seems I am to live the war in Virginia, but as I stated before, I am at a field hospital, not directly right on a battlefield. That, my dear, may change. I regret to say, the Union is losing too many surgeons on the battlefields trying to assist the wounded. I have learned being a doctor doesn't save you from the Rebels. Doctors are also being taking prisoner and being killed right along other soldiers.

The battles are increasing. I have been keeping an ear out for any battles in your area. The only news that I have heard is of the Union trying to take back Fort Sumter. I will say, your Rebel soldiers are winning many battles and are looking strong.

I have heard of battles moving on north up to my home, but my father should be safe. I do believe that both the North and South are shocked at how long and difficult this war has been. Unfortunately, both sides are stubborn and I'm afraid this will go on for a while.

My dear, I miss you more and more. Time may heal all wounds, but for the heart, it causes more pain. It seems our life together is interrupted and we will have to wait. The only honorable thing to do is what we are doing. It is too late to run away now, so we must be patient.

I see in my mind Bella Oak coming to life with the spring. I dream of the time I stand on her great verandah overlooking the grand plantation. I have heard stories, though, that the fields of the South are standing bare and many plantation homes have been destroyed. I pray you and Bella Oak are safe.

Please keep your father, Benjamin, and Terrance near, but if the inevitable happens, please my dear, run and hide away from your home. It can be replaced, but you can't be. Sometimes, I am so filled with worry about your family that I could go out of my mind. Be safe, my love, not sorry.

The night is growing dark and I can hear the moans of pain and anguish coming from the tents lined up outside. The tents are like ghosts with the breeze softly flapping their cloth in the wind. Many nights, I have wished that I was able to shout to Heaven and run as fast as I could, not stop until I am in South Carolina and at your home, never looking back.

Men that are able are standing around with their crutches telling tales of their bloody battles and losing their friends with the memories that will live with them the rest of their lives. I have seen a few, as I feared I might, go insane with the death of so many. The strong young lads are crying and curling up like babies; others sit with a blank, far-away look on their faces, trying to escape what is in their minds.

I have to try and keep my sanity and maybe that is why I share so much with you. The sick and wounded men tell their tales, and it does seem to help. You, my love, stay safe and I will dream tonight of our love and seeing you again someday. Goodnight.

With my love always,

Andrew

She laid the letter along with the others. She worried so about Andrew and now her father, as well. She was glad in one way that Andrew wouldn't be getting her letters, because she did not want to worry him about her father being away while Yankees were camped on Bella Oak.

Benjamin reported each morning what he had learned during the night. The poor boy was running without very much sleep. He was getting a small taste of a soldier's life.

The first of April arrived and the Union soldiers that were camped down by the river left and new ones came with more news of battles and more stories of missing families. Fighting had increased, no doubt. However, Benjamin and Olivia were more concerned with the Yankees that were near. It was so difficult on the two of them hearing the tales from the Union soldiers of so many Rebel soldiers dying.

Ruth was becoming feeble as worry was overcoming her. No one had seen Ruth like this. She was absolutely consumed with depression.

Mama Bea was apprehensive, "I shor hope yo' father comes home soon. Miss Ruth is in bad shape."

Olivia and Benjamin cringed knowing their mother couldn't deal with the knowledge that Yankees were on Bella Oak. They would sit with their mother and talk of times of the past trying to bring a smile to her face, but her dead eyes only wanted to see those green eyes of her William.

Early before sunrise on April twenty second, Tuesday morning Benjamin came running in yelling, "Olivia, Terrance, get up!"

Olivia grabbed a quilt, wrapped it around her, and ran down the stairs as fast as she could.

"What in tarnation is going on? Massa Benjamin quits, stops that yelling, ya hear?" called out Mama Bea as she turned and ordered, "Miss Olivia, gets up to yo' room and dress."

"Benjamin what is it," called out Terrance slipping on his boots hopping along from the back of the house.

"I heard the Yankees talking," Benjamin announced as he began catching his breath.

"Yankees!" yelled Mama Bea, fanning herself with her apron.

"Hush, Mama Bea, you might wake Mother!" Olivia declared, patting the terrified woman.

"The Yankees are planning a sneak attack on Charleston this Friday!" Benjamin hurried into the office. "Friday, there are more troops coming in to join the ones along the river.

"Oh, Benjamin that has to be jest braggart talk. The Union wouldn't dare try to take over Charleston, would they?" questioned Olivia tightening her grip on the quilt.

"I'm afraid so! They will be able to catch our boys off guard. They are planning to burn Charleston to get back at the Confederates, and they are convinced they can win. They say they are going to show Southerners a few things. Many of our Rebels have been sent to Virginia, not leaving many down here to defend Charleston. Furthermore, I am sorry, Olivia, they were telling of more fighting up in Virginia."

"Andrew told me that in his letter. I understand, but Benjamin…Father is there. What can we do to save him?" Olivia begged, standing shaking in her bare feet.

"I'm going to Charleston to warn him. Terrance, go see if Star Bright has been shod. I told your father yesterday that the horse had a limp. I'm sure he has efficiently taken care of a loose shoe by now."

"Benjamin," Olivia began, "this is so dangerous for you, and the Yankees might see you on the road. I don't know if you should go."

"I have thought about that and I know a shortcut that Big John and I took one summer when we went to Charleston. We stopped and hunted traveling through the countryside. I'm going that way, hopefully, out of sight."

"Benjamin," Olivia said, "you're soaking wet."

"Yep, it's misty out there and chilly, a drizzly rain, not fit to be out, but I must warn Father. I have to go upstairs and change clothes. Get me some food and fill my canteen before I depart. I will be leaving as soon as I finish preparing. Time is of the essence."

"I's fix yo' some food, Massa Benjamin," Mama Bea turned and swished her large body around leaving the room. "Yankees on Bella Oak," she kept mumbling.

"Benjamin," tears began to fall down Olivia's face, "I'm so worried about Father and now you." The quilt quivered with Olivia's body trembling underneath.

"You get dressed and I will see you in a few minutes. We will be fine and I will bring Father home safe," Benjamin declared with a determined voice. He turned running up the stairs taking two steps at a time.

She followed behind hurrying to her bedroom. The quilt dropped to the floor as she slipped on her clothes.

Annie looked up with tired eyes, "What is the yelling all about?"

"It's jest Benjamin," Olivia whispered softly. "Don't worry; go back to sleep."

The young girl rolled over pulling the quilts up around her head and fell back to sleep.

Benjamin stopped by the room. He quietly moved into the room leaning down kissing Annie on the forehead.

"Sleep my little angel," he whispered.

Olivia followed him out of the room, but they stopped. "You have to come home to me. I can't make it without you."

"I will. It'll jest be quiet for a while with me gone," he teased. "You'll see, I will be back soon if only to irritate you, sister dear." He leaned over hugging Olivia. Neither of them wanted to let go.

He held onto her arm as they descended the long staircase together. There, standing at the bottom, was Terrance and Mama Bea.

Benjamin took the supplies of food from Mama Bea and she reached over with her large arms hugging the boy she had raised from birth as her own.

Terrance stepped up and they shook hands but then hugged. "Let me go with yo', Benjamin."

"No, it's like Father said, someone has to stay here to defend Bella Oak. Plus, you have your family here. I will be fine, my friend, and will see you later."

He hugged Olivia and kissed her on her forehead. He had grown so much taller the last couple of years. She looked up into her brother's face with those eyes narrowing staring down.

"I love you, and I will be back soon."

"What about Mother?" she questioned.

"I gave her a hug before I left last night and told her how much I love her. Let her rest," he said turning to leave.

"My father has Star Bright ready to go," Terrance added stepping out onto the verandah with him.

Olivia stood at the door peering out into the cold, drizzly, early morning with big, horizontal, puffy clouds almost hiding the sun. The morning colors were radiating around the clouds' edges, giving off an eerie scene as if they were announcing danger to Charleston.

She watched as Benjamin leaped up on his horse, sitting straight and tall just as their father had taught him. He waved goodbye, riding off down the path through the oaks and out of the safety of Bella Oak. He was on his mission; a man's work lay ahead of him.

She stood there and could see Benjamin in her mind, riding out across the land hiding from the Yankees. This was so dangerous and he was alone. She knew Andrew said loneliness was the hardest part of being away. She said a prayer and couldn't move paralyzed with the emptiness inside of her. Terrance's hand gently took her arm, pulling her back into the foyer.

Terrance kept watch with a few other men who had stayed. He stationed the men around the plantation home and gave each of them a small, bamboo, Catawba Indian whistle on a leather cord to wear around their necks. If they saw or heard anything, they were to blow the three-note widgeon call to alarm everyone.

The women were to stay inside or close to an outside door. Mama Bea knew the widgeon call and was able to whistle it herself. Olivia spent almost an entire afternoon getting Mama Bea to teach her the whistle. She finally was able to make the widgeon sound using the bamboo whistle, but she could never whistle it like Mama Bea could.

That night, Olivia laid her fork down by her plate. She just couldn't eat much at supper that night. The silence and feeling vulnerable were wearing on her. She decided to go to her room early.

She sat at her window looking out into the darkening night with the glowing of the sun sinking once more behind the clouds, wondering where her brother might be and whether he was out of harm's way.

Friday came and she was numb with fear, believing the fighting was occurring. The one big question in her mind was, had Benjamin been able to warn her father and the others. Her stomach was tight and her emotions were heavy with worry. She could intuitively feel something was wrong.

She stood quietly looking out on Bella Oak. It was if the plantation was crying. The wind was blowing hard, whistling through the pine needles, and making an eerie sound like a banshee.

Chapter Eighteen
"Benjamin"

The next afternoon she was in the office sitting with Annie as they watched Baby Benjamin play on the floor with blocks. She heard a ruckus out front. She hurried to the window and saw riders coming down the path and her father was in the lead. Yes, they were all right. She ran out onto the verandah. She could see behind her father was Big John sitting tall in the saddle. Thank God, they were safe. Her heart stopped…

Behind Big John was a body lying over the saddle of Star Bright with the Southern Cross flag over it. She screamed racing out into the yard. William leaped off his horse and grabbed her. Her body slumped in his arms with her legs giving way. She stared up into his drawn face that didn't have any more tears. He nodded his head, yes. Terrance stood to the side, his body shaking.

Big John and Jonas lifted Benjamin's limp body gently from the horse and carried him into the house to a room in the back. Some of the slaves who were standing around jumped onto their horses and raced off to tell the news that Benjamin Bellamead had been killed by the Yankees.

"Terrance, my son," William managed to say, putting his hand on the young man's shoulder and seeing tears running down his dark face. "Are you alright?"

Terrance wiped his face, "I will be Sir. I have to be."

"See to Olivia for me," he said when he saw Annie shivering holding onto Baby Benjamin leaning on the doorframe of the office.

Sadie came running up grabbing the baby. Annie didn't move and William held onto her. Mama Bea stood at the door with tears running down her old, worn face, she had lost her baby boy, too.

William looked over at the old woman, "Please see to Annie, I have to go to Ruth."

"Massa William," she stopped him, sniffling, catching her breath, "Miss Ruth isn't doing well and this is going to be so hard on her."

"It's hard on all of us."

As tears came in his eyes, he patted Mama Bea on the back walking past nodding his head. William took two steps at a time up the staircase disappearing into his bedroom. They heard a scream and then it was quiet.

Joseph threw open the front door, "Olivia, this isn't true, is it?"

"Yes, Joseph," she looked at the young boy standing trying to be so brave.

She walked over to him wrapping her arms around him. He broke down and began to sob.

"Why, Benjamin?"

"I don't know. I feel like life is being sucked clean out of me."

She knew her feelings about something being wrong had been correct. She didn't know how she could go on without her brother. They were so alike, and it was if she had lost a part of herself.

William walked slowly down the stairs. He stepped off the last stair. "Mama Bea, please go see to Ruth. She needs you now."

"Yes, Massa William," replied the old woman looking up into those sad green eyes.

"Father, what happened," cried out Joseph.

"Your brother died a hero. He came to Charleston and told us of the Union strike. We were able to get the news to General P.G.T. Beauregard. Our soldiers were able to counter the Union soldiers, commanded by Major General Quincy Gillmore and were capable of holding them back. Before the battle, one of the men brought Benjamin a grey uniform. They were all so proud of him. He had his portraiture made," he reached into his pocket. "Here," he said, handing Olivia a picture of a young Rebel soldier, her brother. Benjamin stood proud with his eyes staring so intensely, those eyes she had said goodbye to just a few days ago. He had been a Rebel soldier, just as he wanted.

"We all prepared for the battle, determined that the Yankees weren't going to burn Charleston. We were going to win, no matter what it took.

"John and I positioned ourselves and Benjamin took a spot to the side of us. The shots began as the Union soldiers approached, but our Rebels fought back pushing them away with haste. One young Union soldier, not much older than Benjamin, somehow made his way into our line. He lifted his gun to shoot me. Benjamin yelled trying to warn me and the man turned to him and fired.

"I heard the shot as it rang out, and I froze seeing Benjamin fall to the ground. My heart stopped along with his that morning. I bent down and he looked up at me. Instead of being concerned about himself, he was concerned of all of us, especially you, Olivia. He told me to tell you to not be sad, that he would always be watching over Bella Oak and would never leave.

"He didn't suffer, as he lay back in my arms, closed his eyes, and exhaled a soft breath. He died a hero, jest as he lived his life always thinking of others. Benjamin fought hard, but without him warning us, many more would have died including me and John." They all stood in shock as he turned to leave the room.

"I have a funeral to plan," he said walking out the door with his head bent down.

Sunday, April twenty-seventh, 1863 the Bellamead family was standing out in their small cemetery surrounded by old live oaks with Spanish moss swaying in the light breeze. One small militia of men, the ones who had been saved by Benjamin came to pay their respects for the young hero.

The preacher began, "We are standing here saying goodbye to a brave young man, Benjamin Randell Bellamead, a hero who saved many lives risking his own, a young man who was loved by all. He was full of life and will be sorely missed. We will always remember his laughter as it rang out when he ran up telling one of his stories. He shore was a storyteller. His innocence of youth was robbed, and circumstances required him to step up, practically overnight, to manhood. He quickly became a man destined to save many on the sad day April twenty-fifth. I look out among so many of our Confederate soldiers standing here because of his selfless act. God bless them and take this young soul into Heaven to be rewarded."

He began reading familiar *Bible* verses, and then everyone sang *Amazing Grace* with Big John leading them.

At the end, Big John stepped up and began to sing *I Am a Rebel Soldier and Far From My Home*. The soldiers sang along with him and their voices rose out over the hills of Bella Oak. Olivia stood strong hoping some of the Yankees were near hearing the song sung by the Confederate soldiers.

Everyone walked by to say how sorry they were and to say goodbye to Benjamin. With tears in their eyes, the boys from the county each took turns offering condolences, and some embraced Olivia.

Hansford leaned down, "We won't forget him and Albert. They will always be with us," he whispered kissing her forehead.

Her eyes were unblinking, but not seeing, as they all passed by. Then it was her time to say goodbye to her brother.

Her trembling hand softly touched the casket that was draped with the Southern Cross flag, a symbol of battle with bright red, a blue cross, and many stars. The cool wind was blowing through the bare limbs that had started to bud out with golden fuzz. The air was fragrant with the freshness of spring.

She took a deep breath. How could she say goodbye to Benjamin? He had been her protector since they were little. Even as a small child, he had always come to her rescue.

"Oh, my Benjamin, my brother, I can't say goodbye. I will never say goodbye to you. You will always be in my heart. I won't forget your love, never. You are part of me. There is such a void in my heart."

Her body shook trying to take in air. Her throat tightened choking the life out of her.

"I promise I will continue on, but I am so lonely now. I do hope you have found peace, my brave young soldier. I know you will always stand guard over Bella Oak and will always be here with me. All I have to do is look around. You have left your mark on every inch of this plantation, and you have left it on my heart too."

She stroked the casket one last time and turned back to Annie and Joseph. There were only three of them now, the children of Bella Oak.

Chapter Nineteen
"More Battles"

Without Benjamin, the days were quiet at Bella Oak. He made the plantation come to life. Olivia woke each morning with sorrow in her heart and each night she lay in bed with the quietness becoming so deafening, she wanted to scream. The sounds of Benjamin stomping up the steps while Mama Bea hollered at him and then her mother yelling from the Parlor, "Benjamin Randell Bellamead what are you doing?" had become quiet, too quiet.

Terrance's eyes were sad, losing his best friend in the world. He would stand holding Baby Benjamin tightly looking out on Bella Oak. Mama Bea wasn't even yelling at her when she would do something that wasn't ladylike. Poor Annie, without her older brother to see to her, was devastated since she didn't have the courage of Olivia.

Of course, there was Joseph. Although a young boy, he believed he had to take charge just like Benjamin. William had caught him spying on the Union soldiers down by the river, which worried everyone. Joseph was too young to understand the consequences of his game, possibly a shot through the heart.

Ruth, now, that was another story. The tiny woman's soul had been broken and Olivia understood more of what Andrew had said in one of his letters, that there was a fine line between sanity and insanity. Ruth stayed in her bedroom. She sat by the window looking out still believing Benjamin would come home to her.

The weeks continued on with William and few of the slaves who had remained planting cotton out in the field. They stayed close to the plantation home. He had to try to get some normalcy back into his life, but his face was drawn, knowing his Bella Oak would never be the same. His beloved Plantation was dying right in front of him, as his son did.

Olivia took over for her mother at the home. She saw to the meals and the care of everyone. With the warmer weather, time came to plant the garden so they would have some vegetables to eat. Ruth had always seen to the garden. She had the green thumb, not Olivia. With the help of Sadie, the two young girls got the job done. At least they would be able to eat for a while.

William had learned that many of his cattle had been butchered by the Yankees, leaving a very small herd. He and Big John had brought what was left up to pasture just out from the house so that they could see them.

Supplies in town had dwindled and coffee, flour, and sugar had become scarce. Olivia was proud of Benjamin for gathering up supplies the last time he went into town, but she knew they wouldn't last long.

Weeks and then months went by without news from Andrew, causing Olivia more stress. Her heart was breaking.

She kept remembering Benjamin's body lying there in front of her. When she would close her eyes, she would see Andrew's face instead of Benjamin's lying so still. It was as if the war was trying to drive her insane. The only savior was she was busy running Bella Oak during the day, but at night, the devil of darkness swooped into her thoughts until sleep came.

"Father," she looked into his worried eyes as he rode up, jumping down from his horse, "what is the news of the Yankees down by the river?"

"Olivia," he shook his head, "my sweet daughter, I grieve so that I have to burden you."

He ascended the steps looking down at his boots. His face had aged in the last few months. This war was taking the life right out of him. His shoulders were slumped, not straight anymore. He was exhausted from the hard work and worry.

"The Union troops are growing and the news…" he stopped and heaved a big sigh, "…the news is that there has been many massive battles in Virginia. Our Rebels did win, but the loss was heavy on both sides."

"Father," she cried out, "what do you mean massive battles."

"The men called it the Chancellorsville campaign and it seems that over a hundred thousand men fought in those battles. The Rebel infantries were strong with General Robert E. Lee and General Thomas Jackson leading them. The Union boys down by the river were angry because Lee and Jackson divided their troops, sneaking up on them and leaving the Union off guard. Their only liberator was the darkness.

Many Union soldiers died that first of May. There also were many commanders that died during that campaign. One I remember hearing about from you was General Whipple of the third division III Corps. Of course my information was one sided and I'm sure exaggerated."

"Father," she panicked jumping out of her chair, "that is Andrew's commander." Her body slumped being consumed with fear. "That is why I haven't heard from Andrew. He has been in battle."

She collapsed down in her chair.

"I'm sorry to worry you," William proclaimed with his body tensing. "When will this devastation ever end?"

He moaned and turned to the door. Olivia wanted a distraction so she went to the garden.

The hot summer sun was blaring down on her as she worked the garden with sweat running down her face. She wiped her forehead with her sleeve of her worn, stained dress. She didn't look like a Southern belle now. Her once soft white hands were rough, dry, and cracking from the hard work. She kept her bonnet on trying to shield her face, but the freckles were growing across her nose. She wasn't worried about her looks as long as they all a sufficient amount of food.

Each day she would bring in enough vegetables from the garden to can for the winter. She hoped to have enough food to feed everyone who had stayed, which now had dwindled to a small few. Big John, Jeremiah, James, Jonas, Terrance, and Mama Bea along with their families, were the only slaves who had stayed on Bella Oak. That wasn't a lot to run a large plantation.

Chapter Twenty
"More Letters"

The end of June, Terrance came running to the side of the home. He raced over to the garden where Olivia was gathering tomatoes.

"Olivia, hurry come here!" he yelled.

She dropped the vegetables wrapped in her apron onto the ground and ran to the front of the home.

"Terrance, what is it?"

"Good news," he yelled waving an envelope in the air.

She sighed with the anxiousness leaving. She took the letter in her hands and could see it was Andrew's handwriting. She still feared a letter coming from another surgeon telling her a sad fate, a letter with someone else's handwriting.

She sat down in the shade of the verandah and carefully tore open the envelope. She gently lifted out the letter with her dirty fingers.

DIANN SHADDOX

Sunday, May seventeenth, 1863

My dearest Olivia, my precious love,

It is another sad night as I write to you. My world has once more been turned upside down. My days of working in the field hospital stopped the end of April. I left with my division and commander General Amiel Whipple. Our division joined forces with General Joseph Hooker in Chancellorsville, Virginia.

I sit here by the campfire with so much grave news. The battle began with the Rebels catching us off guard. Hearing the Rebel cry and the sounds of gunshots being fired shook me from the inside out. Whilst our men sat eating and relaxing at night, they were attacked.

My body was paralyzed with fear watching men dropping all around me to the ground. I began my duties trying to save as many as I could. Ultimately, the body count grew faster than my hands could work.

As my hands explored the soldier's wounds, my mind kept replaying that only a few minutes before they were laughing and having a good time. In our makeshift hospital, the amputations have piled up. Body parts are actually being carted and buried nearby in people's yards. I am constantly standing in and walking in blood from soldier to soldier. It is nauseating.

Then the unmentionable happened. My commander General Whipple was shot in the stomach by a Confederate sharpshooter. He had fallen from his horse and had lost a lot of blood by the time he was brought to me. I reached into his warm body pulling out the round ball with the knowledge that he wouldn't make it.

My friend Chaplain Eli stood nearby with his face stern. Without words being spoken, I shook my head and he understood. He gave the commander his last rites as I struggled to repair the damage. General Whipple was sent to Washington, DC, where he died three days later.

The popping noise of the gunfire pounds in my head and the ground shakes from the cannon blasts, which only end with darkness coming on. However, the moans and cries resonating from the battlefield never end.

With the light of a lantern, I have worked through the night trying to save a few. There are so many wounded and not enough time to reach them. Our men who had not been wounded began trying to take the wounded to the nearest field hospital, but they were so outnumbered by the dying.

I, my dear, at the moment, I am safe sitting here writing you. By the grace of God, He must have a purpose for my life, though death surrounds me. I think of you and know I have to endure, but it is getting difficult. I am just tired and the moans of pain pierce my mind.

I did hear news that other leaders lost their lives during the battles, Union General Berry in the second division died during the battle. News has circulated that the Rebels lost one of their strong commanders. I don't have the details but General Thomas Jackson died May tenth after being mortally wounded, along with another commander, General Paxton. The Confederates won this battle, but at a steep cost.

My dear, the stories of our Union soldiers camping out down in the South have grown. Small militias are being position in strategic areas, so please, be on the lookout.

I still hope Benjamin has not left Bella Oak and everyone is safe. I miss hearing your stories and tales from your letters, but I do dream I will see you soon.

My hands are beginning to shake from fatigue. I have worked nonstop for weeks. I fear my hands will fail me in the operating room. Our Lord's faithfulness has been gracious unto me, and I pray that He shall continue to be.

I long for our arms to be wrapped around one another. I have to see those green eyes of innocence and feel those soft lips. My dreams are what keep me alive.

Yet again, I apologize for worrying you so. Now that I have parlayed to you, I will try to rest.

With my love always,

Andrew

She sat back in her chair feeling relieved. She knew that Benjamin's death would be too hard on Andrew and it might send him into a deeper depression. That piece of information she would keep until the day he came home. She sighed now understanding the hell on earth that he was going through. Remembering her brother's body was enough death for her. How could Andrew stand operating on so many, as more lay dead around him?

Chapter Twenty-One
"William"

The first of July was upon Bella Oak and it was challenging for the family. There would be no picnic this year.

Olivia sat dreaming of the picnic just a couple years ago. She could vision Andrew standing so debonair asking her to dance and them twirling on the dance floor. She closed her eyes hearing the music flow through the hills feeling Andrew's soft hands holding onto her. It seemed now she only had memories.

This war was continuing on and on destroying everyone and everything. She shook with anger. She looked down at her own hands cracked, rough, and dry. Here she was sitting in an old faded dress. There wouldn't be any more new frilly dresses at Bella Oak for a long time, maybe never. A lone tear ran down her face.

The day was unearthly hot for some reason and the rains had held off the past few days. The sun was scorching the ground.

Joseph and Terrance were out patrolling near the home, watching and listening for any signs of the Yankees coming in the vicinity of the plantation. Big John and William had gone to see to what cattle they had left in the backfield.

She sat for a few minute resting on the verandah, drifting off dreaming of the picnic. She could see Benjamin grinning when she came up the hill from the spring after spending time with Andrew. She was so sad that Benjamin had not lived to find his one true love.

Her thoughts were interrupted by Joseph, "Olivia! Olivia!"

There to the side was Big John with William thrown over his shoulder. Blood was running down Big John's back. Terrance jumped up on his horse and took off into town to find the doctor. Joseph ran to Big John as he stepped up onto the porch. Olivia opened the front door. Her heart was beating so fast she couldn't catch her breath.

"Mama Bea, come quick!" she screamed.

Big John laid William onto the cot in the back room of the home. The same cot they had placed Benjamin before his burial. Mama Bea began yelling out orders. Sadie came into the room carrying a bowl of water and many rags. She undid William's shirt, blood oozed out flowing onto the cot.

"Oh, I wish yo' mother could help. She would knows what to do."

"We can see to him," Olivia said getting down on her knees by the cot. She began to clean the wound and put pressure on it to slow down the blood loss.

"Please God, let him live and let Terrance get here soon with the doctor."

The pressure was slowing the flow of blood. Her hands were covered in red.

"Miss Olivia, if the doctor doesn't gets here soon, wez will has to get that shot out."

"Oh, Andrew, I wish you were here," she whispered softly pressing down tight on the wound.

It seemed like hours, but it wasn't when she heard a buggy riding up outside. She finally caught her breath. Dr. Holt hurried into the room. He stopped and puckered his mouth with his head leaning to the side.

"Let me see, Olivia." He squatted down and removed the blood soaked rag. "We have to get that shot out."

He began to pour some antiseptic and clean the wound. He pulled from his bag a few instruments and his old hands reached into the body of her father, just as Andrew would have. Dr. Holt's skilled hand pulled the round ball out of her father and laid it to the side. Queasiness was overcoming her. She became pale.

"Olivia, don't faint on me, girl." Dr. Holt stated with concern. "I don't need two patients."

"Yes, I will be fine," she assured, getting her composure back.

He busily stitched up the wound and then he carefully placed a sterile dressing over it.

"Now, Olivia, you will have to see to changing the dressing for me. I won't be able to come back often, the wounded are growing, and I'm traveling all over the county. I will leave you some sterile dressings and send Terrance if you see any infection. I'm not going to lie to you girl, William has lost a lot of blood and the wound is very serious. I guess we are lucky that I was too old to be sent to fight. I have heard stories from William of your young man seeing to the wounded. Regardless of the side he is on as a doctor, I do feel sorry for him.

The doctor shook his head, overwhelmed, and taking in a deep breath.

"My poor, caring William. A kinder man, I'll never meet. He wouldn't hurt a soul," he said softly patting William's arm.

Olivia could see the worry in the old doctor's eyes understanding William's chances were very low to survive. She looked back at everyone by the door. They were all looking to her for support, but her heart was heavy.

"Thank you, Dr. Holt," she said with an exasperated sigh.

She reached over to the older man seeing his heart breaking as he stared at his friend lying there so quietly. She knew it wasn't any easier being a doctor watching death. She stood, turned, and walked to the foyer.

"Olivia," Dr. Holt asked, "what happened?"

She shook her head she didn't know.

"Dr. Holt, I nos," Big John commented with his clothes soaked in blood.

"What happened, Big John?" asked Olivia.

"We wuz out to the back pasture checkin' on the cattle. I seen a calf that had wondered off an went to help. Massa William was seein' to the others. I heard a shot and run up the hill an there in front of him was three mens. One damn Yankee, and two scalawags lookin' to steal whatever they could. William shots one and the man fell off his horse, the other lifted his gun and Massa William pulled out his pistol shoots him dead. Before he could shoot again, the other mans shot him. I raised mys gun and shot that man. The horses bucked and rans leavin' all the mens on the ground. I picks up Massa William an carrys him home. I should have been there with him to protect him, I jest worn't close enough."

"You did what you could, Big John," assured Dr. Holt, patting the large man on the arm. "Olivia those bodies will have to be buried before anyone else sees them. You can't take any chances."

"Those gawd dam, yellow-bellied Yankees! My father was no soldier; he was no threat to them. I might have to go put another shot in them to be sure their dead!" cried out Olivia.

"Olivia, honey," Dr. Holt took her by the shoulders, "listen to me. You must remain calm. It won't do for you to go flyin' off the handle now."

Olivia nodded her head in agreement. Then she took a deep breath.

"Dr. Holts, doan yous' worries none. Terrance and Jonas, they's seein' to them dead Yankees," answered Big John.

"Good, I must be going, I have many others to see today," Dr. Holt added overwhelmed. "Many Rebel soldiers are coming home wounded. Send Terrance if you have any problems. Honey, I reckon you will be seeing to Bella Oak on your own, with your father laid up and your mother not doing so well. If you require any help, let me know."

"Yes, Sir, I will, and I will be fine. I jest wish Andrew would come home soon," she replied solemnly.

"Big John, you take care of her." The old man looked up at the huge man. But, both of them looked worn out.

She watched as Dr. Holt's buggy pulled down the path to the gates. She saw dark clouds in the sky rolling in. She gripped one of the large pillars supporting the verandah. Suddenly, loud thunder rolled and rain began pelting down. The lightning crackled in the sky and the thunder continued to boom, shaking the plantation home.

She closed her eyes as the thunder grew and could see Andrew out in the battle with the canons and guns firing around him. She saw how much blood one man lost and couldn't comprehend hundreds and maybe thousands of bodies covered in blood.

Her body started to shake, but not from her images. The thought that she was losing her family one at a time hit her hard.

She had to keep everyone safe, but how? Now, not only were the Union soldiers on Bella Oak but also scalawags were ready to steal from them. *How are people like that stopped?*

The rain continued to fall cleansing the ground knowing the rain and time would erase all evidence of the shooting and the graves. Tomorrow she would ask Big John to finish moving the cattle and horses or whatever was left next to the home.

No one was to venture off alone anymore and she would have Terrance and Jeremiah guarding near the house. She touched her pistol knowing she wouldn't hesitate to use it.

Olivia pulled up a chair by her father and sat down. She watched the man so like her taking in shallow breaths. The light flickering from the lamp was glowing on his pale face leaving signs of pain and anguish. She gently wiped his face wishing he would look up at her and tell her everything would be all right.

"Father, please don't worry. Just get well. I will see to everything. We will be fine. You rest and get better," she softly whispered to him.

"Miss Olivia, I will sits wit him. Yous' gets some rest," Mama Bea pleaded, looking at the worn young face in front of her.

"I am fine Mama Bea. Will you see to Annie and Joseph for me tonight?"

"Yes' am, but youse calls me if yo' need me, yous' heres."

"I will," don't worry so Mama Bea. Now you get some rest and you can help me tomorrow.

The old black woman stood in the doorway looking back at the young girl she had raised. Mama Bea knew Olivia had grown into a woman with the responsibility of this huge plantation.

The next morning about four o'clock, William opened his eyes. His green eyes stared straight at her.

"My dear, you shouldn't be sitting in that hard chair. You can't get any rest like that."

"Father," she gently called out getting down on her knees beside him.

"It's not good is it," he whispered trying to catch his breath with his chest rattling.

"No," she had never been able to lie to him and wasn't starting now. "You lost a lot of blood and you are the one who should rest."

She smiled at him, trying to scold him in a teasing matter like he used to do to her.

"Now, young lady, I'm still Master of the home," he smiled back, "but it seems you are right now. I am tired. Does your mother know?"

"No, we didn't tell her about you. That is why you are in this back room. Father, I don't think she could cope with this."

He closed his eyes for a minute.

"Father, you rest. Do you need anything?"

"No, but you also get some rest and get out of that hard chair. At least get a cot in here."

"I will. I have to change your bandages soon. Mama Bea made you some broth to sip on. It will make you feel better."

"Oh," he sighed.

"If you're in too much pain, I can get some whisky."

"No, my sweet Olivia, I should be taking care of you."

"I reckon, it's my time for a while, Father. Please don't worry so. It's like Benjamin said, we are so like you. I will be able to see to things. You know, I feel Benjamin here helping."

"Olivia, it was strange, when those men rode up on me. I heard someone yell to warn me. A warning sounded, "Shoot the Yankee…Don't wait!""

She stared at him with a wondering look.

"Yes, the voice sounded like Benjamin's, and I didn't hesitate to fire," he answered. "Olivia…could it have been?"

"He did say he was going to watch over Bella Oak. I so wish he were here."

"I too, my dear," he said closing his eyes.

She sat back in the chair wondering if Benjamin's spirit was really here on Bella Oak. It somehow made her feel better, not so lonely.

Morning came, she changed William's dressings, and he sipped some broth making her believe all was well. She had work in the garden to see to, vegetables to pick and can for the winter, so she let Mama Bea watch over William.

Olivia went to the garden alone without changing clothing. The garden was particularly fresh after the rain and the vegetables plump and clean. It was ironic, but Olivia found peace in the garden. She wished her whole world could be like it, but it wasn't to be, not while the war raged on.

William seemed to be improving, but was weak. Olivia brought a cot into the room so she would be close at night. The plantation was calm and there weren't any more disturbances or signs of Yankees hiding out. They had moved on, giving her a little breathing space. It had gotten quiet. No letters arrived from Andrew and that worried her. She sat each night watching her father's labored breathing and still could see the struggle on his face.

Saturday night, July eleventh, her father began to moan. She saw in the light of the oil lamp his face was flushed. She gently touched his forehead. It was scorching hot.

"Terrance," she said frantically running down the hallway. She stood at his bedroom door quietly knocking trying not to wake little Benjamin. "Terrance," she called out again.

He opened the door, "Olivia, what is it?"

"It's father, he's burning up, Hurry, go and get Dr. Holt."

He didn't hesitate. He grabbed his boots, raced to the back door, and out of the home. Olivia hurried to Mama Bea's room and knocked.

"Mama Bea, it's Olivia, I need help."

The old woman dressed in her nightclothes came to the door, "Olivia, is it your father?"

"Yes, he's so hot."

"Well, child, get some water and rags," she called out hurrying to William's room.

Olivia carried the dishpan of water and rags into the room.

"Start's wiping him down, we has to get hims cool," Mama Bea called out as she laid the damp rag on William's brow. "Wipe his arms, has yo sent fur the doctor?"

"Yes, Terrance is on his way."

"Miss Olivia, this isn't good." Mama Bea stood up straight shaking her head. "Keeps turning the rags to cool's him."

"Please Father, wake up," Olivia whispered staring down at her father's lifeless body while she continued to lay the cool rags on him.

Terrance and Dr. Holt stepped into the room. She saw the look on the old doctor's face.

Dr. Holt bent down next to William, "I was afraid of this. That dang shot has infected him even with us cleaning the wound."

"But the wound looks fine," Olivia blurted out.

"It's inside of him. Honey, it's not good. Here is some medicine, try and get him to take some. I hope he is strong enough to fight. It is up to his body now. I can't do anymore."

Mama Bea came into the room, "Dr. Holt, here's some coffee fer ya."

"Thank ya, Mama Bea. It's going to be a long day." He nodded his head. "Olivia I will stay here, if you don't mind."

"Thank you," she spoke with tears running down her face. She understood what he meant. He would stay until the end.

The morning light flickered in through the window. William moaned. Olivia leaned near, "Father, please wake up and take some medicine," she whispered.

Those green eyes looked up and the doctor smiled, but their happiness was short lived.

"Benjamin, why are you looking so sad?" he asked looking past Olivia. "Son, we are alright. You have work to see to, chickens to feed, and that cow in the barn needs milking."

"Father," Olivia whispered, "it's me, not Benjamin.

"Yes, Benjamin, I'm fine, but, young man, your face shor' is drawn. You are going to worry your Mother. Did you wipe your boots? They shor' look dirty. I swanny, boy, stop worrying so."

"Olivia," Dr. Holt assured, "he is delirious. He doesn't see you, but for some reason he sees Benjamin. Maybe that is what is on his mind."

Tears ran down Olivia face as she held her father's hand, knowing it wasn't his mind. He did see his son standing by him. She looked around the room. She felt softness on her shoulder like a wisp of air.

She whispered, "Benjamin take care of him. I love you both."

"Son, where are we going," William said softly, holding out his hand. "I can't leave your mother. This will devastate her. I have to stay."

William got quiet and closed his eyes. Then, he briefly rallied.

"Yes Father it's time to go home," William whispered with a sigh, staring past her.

"I love you, father." Olivia leaned over touching his face. "Goodnight," she whispered, never saying goodbye.

William drew his last breath, his body relaxed, and his chest was still.

Dr. Holt looked over, "Olivia he is gone. Rest from this weary world, my friend, and rejoice in the joy of our Lord."

"Oh father, oh father," Olivia mumered.

"Olivia, honey, why did he call out to his father?"

Olivia looked up at the doctor. "His father James died many years ago. It was like he was seeing him, maybe...," she answered.

Hearing sobs coming from the other room, she looked toward the door and Joseph and Annie were standing there. She jumped up and grabbed them. Her world was shrinking. She held onto them for a bit, as they sobbed.

"Mama Bea, see to them. I have to go tell Mother."

"Olivia, I think I should go upstairs with you to see Ruth," Doctor Holt said kindly.

"Yes, thank you."

She let go of Annie and Joseph and solemnly walked up the stairs with Dr. Holt.

"I have some advice, Olivia, about William's cause of death," Dr. Holt said as they ascended the stairs. "I am going to say that he died of pneumonia. No one needs to know he got shot. It could mean life or death for the rest of you if word gets outside of Bella Oaks that you are alone. Promise me you'll instruct the others?" the doctor questioned.

"I understand and I will insist that everyone here says that father died of pneumonia. We'll not breathe a word about the shooting," Olivia stopped in front of her mother's bedroom door.

Her hand reached out turning the doorknob. Then, she and Dr. Holt walked into the room.

Ruth was sitting by the window. Her light blue dress was flowing down to the floor. Her eyes were intense peering out over the plantation. Her body was rigid not moving. Her tiny hands positioned on her lap with a white handkerchief lying under her soft fingers.

Olivia took in a deep breath. She squeezed her hands together tight. "Mother, I have to talk to you."

"I already know, my dear sweet Olivia. Benjamin told me that my sweet William is gone and I am now alone."

"You have us, you aren't alone," Olivia begged, getting down on her knees next to her mother. She could see the resolution in her mother's expression, which penetrated Olivia's heart, breaking it even more.

Ruth looked up. "Dr. Holt, it is a sad day for Bella Oak. Do you remember that Fourth of July picnic when I first came here? William was so proud to show us both off, his beloved plantation and new wife."

Dr. Holt nodded.

"Remember the day right here in that bed when you helped me bring this sweet young girl into the world?" Ruth patted Olivia gently on the arm with a glint of a smile overtaking the drawn face.

"Yes, Ruth," Dr. Holt smiled, "and William almost passed out. Here this strong young man started weaving back and forth, but when you handed him his small pink baby he held her so gently and tight. Ruth, we have to remember the good times and keep his memory alive. It seems you are feeling better."

"My body is weak and my heart is broken. I feel devoid of hope, and my life is futile, but Benjamin is helping me. He is such a strong boy."

Dr. Holt looked over at Olivia then said to Ruth, "Let me give you something to help you rest. It will be a tiring few days, my dear."

He reached over taking Ruth's small hand in his helping her into the bed. She lay back with her light curls wrapping around her drained, pale face, as she finally fell asleep

"Olivia, her mind is going. Does she believe she sees and talks to Benjamin often?" He shook his head worriedly.

"Yes," replied Olivia, "I think she does believe that she can talk to Benjamin."

"Strange how she knew William died! She didn't even know he had been shot?"

Olivia didn't answer. She softly smoothed her mother's beautiful curly hair from her face. She believed Benjamin had really been talking to her mother but she wasn't going to comment about it further.

Chapter Twenty-Two
"Saying Goodbye Again"

Olivia was standing outside in the warm sun as the tall pines blew softly back and forth over her head. Once more she was saying goodbye to someone she loved, her father. She took in a deep breath smelling the sweet scent of summer blending with the fresh wild flowers sprouting up everywhere. This was her father's favorite time of the year. Her eyes scanned the small cemetery that was now filling with family.

Only a few people in the county had been told of William's death, it wasn't the huge gathering that would have joined them in times of the past. They stood quietly listening to the preacher say his words.

"We are standing here today to say goodbye to a long and trusted friend, William Randell Bellamead who had love and compassion for everyone. Anyone who had ever been lucky enough to have met William left that encounter a better person. The legacy he leaves behind is the value of a strong sense of friendship and kindness he always imparted. This, my friends, is a sad day for the world, but William would be the first to tell us to live our lives like he did, not fearing what could be. Dare to hope and dream, that is what he would tell us." The preacher bowed his head and finished his prayer.

Big John stepped up. He began to sing:

> *Amazing Grace, how sweet the sound,*
> *That saved a wretch like me.*
> *I once was lost but now am found,*
> *Was blind, but now I see.*

His voice rose with passion as the man stood singing with his head looking up into the heavens. Tears were running down his heartrending dark face.

When he finished singing, a silence fell over the group and one last prayer was said. Everyone walked up to Olivia to say how sorry they were.

Once the funeral had ended, Olivia took her mother's arm and with small steps led her over to their buggy.

"Olivia," Ruth began with such ease in her voice, "your brother was so angry today. He doesn't understand. He believes this is his fault. William would be so upset at him for thinking that. Talk to him for me, will you?"

"Yes, ma'am, I will," she answered.

Big John stepped up helping them into the buggy. His eyes grew big and he shook his head hearing what Ruth had said about talking to Benjamin as if he were there with them.

The next few weeks, the home was full of sorrow. Ruth wasn't getting any better physically or mentally and she kept talking to Benjamin. Olivia was worried and finally made the decision to send her mother away to her Aunt Violia Walden in Charleston. Maybe she would stop seeing Benjamin. She sent a letter explaining the situation and Aunt Violia agreed some time away from Bella Oak was what Ruth could use.

Ruth seemed to like the idea. This would be a nice visit, not comprehending the war was still going on. Olivia prepared her to leave with Big John escorting her. He was one of the only other people beside Olivia who Ruth felt comfortable with.

Wednesday morning, August the nineteenth quickly arrived. Everyone gave hugs and Olivia had warned her siblings not to cry. This was supposed to be a pleasure trip for their mother. She just hoped she would see her again. They each leaned over hugging the tiny woman. The children could see a faint beauty emerging in the woman whose eyes their father had fallen in love with.

Ruth's small body was posed with assurance in the buggy seat. She never forgot her Southern belle grooming as she kissed her children goodbye.

"Take care, Olivia. Rely on Benjamin; he said he would help you. I will be back soon." She leaned over and kissed her daughter seeing that tiny baby she had held in her arms so long ago.

"Mother, we will be fine. You get to feeling better and I hope you will be home soon. You tell Aunt Violia we send our love."

"I shor' will, goodbye, my loves," she added gently, as Big John grabbed the reins and the horse took off with the clip clopping down the path and out the black iron gates. Olivia bowed her head seeing another loved one leaving Bella Oak.

She turned back to Annie and Joseph. We have work, to do. She began to laugh.

"There are chickens to feed to and cows to milk," she added remembering her father's last words.

Joseph leaned over, "Olivia, I'm old enough to help now and I want to. We'll get this plantation going again."

"Yes, we are going to keep Bella Oak strong. Now get to work!" She clapped her hands, as he ran. She didn't move just stood looking out over the fields that lay with dead brush, not soft white cotton that should be there at this time of year.

A couple of weeks later she sat in the rocker on the verandah. The sky was turning multicolored with the sun setting leaving a peaceful end to the day. She saw a buggy coming up the path. She could see it was Big John and he had a huge grin on his face.

"How was the trip?" she called out. The large man stepped upon the verandah.

"Miss Olivia, my heart is so blessed. Miss Ruth's face became calm when we rode into the city of Charleston. I stays to be shor' she wuz alrights. I wishes yous' could'a seen her."

His head ducked wiping tears, "Miss Ruth wuz back like she wuz before. She even made me sing fur some of the womens in Charleston."

"Well, at least there is some happiness in this world. You look tired, go and get some food, and rest. Thank you, John. I am thankful for that good report," she said gently touching his arm. She turned back to the door pulling it open.

"Good's nights, Miss Olivia and youse needs to rest," he called out, with the buggy rolling slowly to the barn.

Chapter Twenty-Three
"A Union Soldier"

The stories grew in the county of more Union defectors and scalawags hiding out and stealing everything they could take from the plantations. The saving grace was that the story had spread about a few men bragging that they were headed out to take whatever they could from Bella Oak. Then, no one ever heard from them again.

There were all kinds of rumors: some said that they were unsuccessful and headed back up North, some said they were successful and headed out West, some knew that William had died about that time and they suspected foul play, but only Dr. Holt and the Bellameads knew for sure.

Olivia still didn't have any word from Andrew and her heart was overflowing with sorrow. She couldn't sleep at night, even after working hard all day. The plantation was wearing on her. Her body was becoming frail and Mama Bea was bothered. This was too much on one young girl to take on. Joseph and Terrance did all they could, but the responsibility lay on Olivia's shoulders.

The first of October had arrived with the fresh cool air of fall blowing in. That alone was giving her some relief. Working those hot days out in the sun was taking the life out of Olivia.

October the ninth, Olivia was out picking some berries from some bushes that she and Terrance had spotted a few days before when they had checked on the small herd of cattle. She gently placed the berries in her basket. There would be something different for supper tonight, a nice berry pie. She was relaxed and even hummed walking slowly home.

A large hand reached out grabbing her from behind. She let out a blood-curdling scream before the man's other hand covered her mouth. Her basket dropped and berries smashed under their feet. He turned her around and she was staring into a face covered in a beard. He was wearing a worn Union soldier's uniform. Her arms and legs were flying, fighting to try and get her gun, but he was too strong. Queasiness was overcoming her because of the nauseating stench from the man, smelling more like an animal than a man.

"The South shor' does have some fine lookin' women," the Union soldier laughed with Olivia kicking and hitting him.

But, she was too weak to fight someone so strong. She was terrified of what was about to happen. The man's eyes grew wide. His grip loosened and he dropped to the ground like a lead weight. A sword was sticking out of his back.

Her legs were wobbly as she ran but she wasn't stopping hearing the crunching of the leaves on the ground behind her. She couldn't catch her breath trying to scream.

A voice yelled out, "Stop…Olivia!"

She slowed her pace. She turned around. There hurrying to her was a man dressed in a Union soldier's uniform. He grabbed her. She stared into those eyes of the man she had fallen in love so long ago at the Fourth of July picnic. Her body became limp. He slipped his arms under her lifting her up walking through the field to the grand house.

Seeing a Yankee carrying Olivia, Mama Bea whistled out the three-note Catawpa warning call.

Terrance yelled, "Don't move or I will shoot. Put that young girl down."

"My son, I'm not going to put Miss Olivia down. Now you put that gun away and help me," Andrew assured.

"Andrew!" screamed Annie running down the steps of the home. "Olivia, is she alright?"

"Yes, let me get her inside," he replied.

"Her dress is torn. What happened?" Annie questioned, following him into their bedroom.

"A Union soldier attacked her out in the back pasture near the fence by a large clump of trees," he looked up at Annie. "I had to kill him with my sword. My first kill of the war!"

He tenderly laid Olivia down in her bed. He checked her vital signs, but she had fainted dead away and was more exhausted than anything else.

"Annie, you see to her. She will be fine. Just a little rest is all she needs. Come on, son," he said to Terrance, walking to the door. "My name is Andrew," he added looking at the young black man still holding onto his gun.

"You is Andrew!" he exclaimed with a grin coming on his face. "I has brought many letters to Miss Olivia from you, but not lately."

"I will tell my story later. Now, put the gun away."

"Sorry," he said overwhelmed, slipping the gun into his holster.

"Where are William and Benjamin? Don't tell me Benjamin has left for war," Andrew asked walking down the stairs.

"No Sir," the young man answered shaking his head.

"Andrew," hollered Joseph, running into the house.

"My goodness, you shor' have grown, my boy," Andrew reached out his hand.

"I'm fourteen almost fifteen, old enough to go fight. Where's Olivia?"

"She passed out on me, I guess too much shock and work."

"She has been though a lot, Andrew."

"Where is your father?"

"Andrew," Joseph answered, grabbing his arm, "Father was killed."

"What!" Andrew fell against the wall. "What happened?"

"A damn Yankee and two scalawags tried to steal some cattle and father fought them. He killed two and Big John killed the other, but father was shot and the infection from the shot killed him." Joseph finished with his eyes fixed on the Union soldier standing in front of him.

"Then where is Benjamin?"

"He was killed too in Charleston. Father and Big John had gone to Charleston to help some men. Benjamin overheard of an attack from some Union soldiers camped down by the river and rode to warn the men. The Confederates did win that battle, but Benjamin was shot and died that day saving many men including Father. A lot has happened over the last few years."

"What about your mother?"

"She is better, but the stress of the war and losing Benjamin and Father was just too much. So, Olivia sent her to stay with Aunt Violia in Charleston."

"Olivia is alright, isn't she?" Andrew questioned concerned.

"Yes, you know her. She has taken on the responsibility of this plantation, but it is wearing on her. Now that you're here, she will be fine," Joseph offered.

"Joseph, I killed a man out near the fence of the back pasture to the side of the house. Someone needs to bury the body. It can't be found. There need to be no traces of the man's ever being here. You understand?"

"Yes," Joseph inserted. "We had to bury the men Father and Big John shot in graves where no one will ever find them."

"I will help. I'm Terrance, by the way" added the young man stepping up. "I will get the shovels."

"Let's go," Andrew insisted. He stopped and patted Joseph on the back, "Go see your sister. I will be back soon."

Later that morning, Andrew walked into the house along with Terrance. He reached over cleaning his hands with Mama Bea smiling.

"Mister Andrew, she's in the office."

He could see the office door was open. The only sound was his boots clicking on the wooden floor as he made his way to the office. He drew in a breath and stepped into the room. There in front of him was the young girl he had left that day on the verandah, his heart was pounding and his mind was swirling.

She turned around. "Andrew, is it really you?" she whispered reaching out her hand.

"Yes," he said pulling her next to him.

She could feel him breathing. He reached up touching her soft face and leaned down kissing and holding her, his Southern dream.

"How?" she questioned.

"It's a long story that I will tell later. First, I have to kiss and hold onto you. I warned you I might not let you go."

"That's not a problem. I hope you never let me go. She snuggled against his body with her hand on his chest feeling his heart beating. "I have worried so much. I can't believe you are really here."

"I'm here and I'm never leaving."

"What about your orders?"

"Shhh, don't talk," he whispered as he kissed her again, squeezing her body against his.

She didn't believe she would ever feel the passion she had only dreamt of for so long. His stomach growled.

"You're hungry. When was the last time you ate?"

"A couple of days ago."

She looked at him worriedly, but not asking any questions.

"Well, it's time. Mama Bea will have lunch ready. Let's go eat. We'll have our entire lives together!"

He leaned over kissing her again looking into those green eyes that were full of passion leading her into the dining room.

There sitting at the table was Joseph, Annie, and Terrance, along with a young dark girl and child.

"This is Terrance and his wife Sadie and this," moving over playing with the little boy, "is Benjamin," she added as she grinned.

"Terrance and I have met. I am charmed to meet you, Sadie and you, young Benjamin." He stood watching Olivia with the boy. "Who else lives here?"

"Big John, Jonas, Terrance's father, Cyrus and all their families. That is it." Olivia added, "Everyone else has left. Many stayed until after father died; I guess they thought Bella Oak was done for."

"I would like the men to meet me in the office to talk after we eat. Then I will tell my story." He sat down at the head of the table with everyone's faces so relieved. Now they weren't alone.

After they said grace, everyone dipped out the watered down beef stew into their bowls and there on their plates was hot cornbread with melted butter. Andrew's eyes studied the ones sitting at the table. He took a few bites of stew and cornbread then laid his spoon down. His stomach had shrunk from doing without very much food. Olivia sat worriedly watching him.

"Andrew, I am concerned about you. You're so thin."

"My dear, I will be fine, now that I'm home, don't worry so," he said sipping his milk.

Terrance stood, "Sir, I will get everyone."

"Thank you, Terrance," Andrew said scooting his chair back staring at the innocent faces at the table. "Olivia, Joseph, you are welcome to join me in the office. My dear Annie and Sadie, you two don't have to be concerned with my story,"

Olivia stood next to him, reaching her arm around him feeling his ribs. She had been so excited earlier that she hadn't noticed he was skin and bones.

Chapter Twenty-Four
"Two Scalawags"

Andrew stepped into the office. Olivia stood by the window. Seeing William's desk by the window made him freeze in his tracks momentarily. He stared down at William's chair.

"This is so hard to realize he is gone. My father is going to be heart-broken. I do have to tell him all of the news, the good," he said with tears brimming in his eyes, "along with the bad."

Terrance and the other men came into the room along with Joseph. Andrew turned his attention to them.

"My friends, I am a deserter from the Union Army. I now am on the run." He dipped his head down, clinching his hands.

"I'm not proud of my status, but I would leave the Union Army again if the situation presented itself.

"My last battle was with Major General George Meade in Pennsylvania, my home state. This was the Gettysburg Campaign beginning in June ending the first of July, at least for me. The injured and dead were massive. I tried quickly working to save as many lives as possible, but the incoming wounded never ceased.

Some injured lay out on the battlefield for as long as forty-eight hours before being taken to the field hospital. I did my job as well as I could leaving the battlefield and moving back to a field hospital.

"Weeks later, I was working on some soldiers who were telling tales that since the Union had won against General Lee that the Confederates were finished. The battles continued, but they believed the war was won. At first, I paid little attention to their talk, but as time marched on, stories arose that the Union was taking over city after city in the South.

"I continued with my work. At the end of the summer, I heard some soldiers bragging that they were going to South Carolina to destroy some of the large plantation homes. They were going to show the Southerners. My heart stopped with the news. I went to my commander to find out the truth. The answer was affirmed.

"I put a plan into action. I began to watch the small militias each preparing to leave. I also prepared; I couldn't stay and let those soldiers harm Bella Oak. I had to warn you, so I set out along with them. I stole a horse. I followed at a distance behind the one group of soldiers, not letting them take notice of me.

"They continued further south riding past a few Confederate camps. However, the men I was following weren't intent on fighting. They only talked of stealing, cleaning out the plantations, and becoming rich after the war. They never noticed me as I just kept my head down.

"When we made it to South Carolina, I feared for Bella Oak. I knew that I had to get help from you to save Bella Oak and some of the other plantations from their strikes. The regiment arrived late last night. After they had fallen asleep early this morning, I saw one soldier sneak out of camp and I followed him. That was the man who attacked you, Olivia, and the one that I killed.

"Now the end of my story is we have to come up with a plan, these men are preparing on arriving here tonight to steal and destroy Bella Oak."

"Andrew, whur's their camp?" asked Big John.

"Down by the river to the east."

"How many?" asked Jonas.

"Twenty-five, now."

"We have to surprise them. They're not expecting us to know about their plan," Cyrus added. "We shor' need to catch them off guard."

"That's correct. If we surround them at their camp, then we can take them. Do you have enough guns?" questioned Andrew.

"Yes Sir," Big John said. "We needs ter gets ready and leaves."

"You get everyone prepared and I will meet you outside in a few minutes," Andrew suggested, looking at the large man.

"I'm shor' glads yo' home, Massa Andrew."

"John, you don't have to call me Master, I'm just Andrew."

He dipped his head, "All right," with a grin emerging. "Thanks ya Mister Andrew."

"Let's go Big John. They want a Southern welcome so let's oblige 'em," Joseph called out.

The men left the office and Andrew turned to Olivia. He wrapped his arm around her and led her to the front door. They stepped out onto the verandah with Joseph stepping up to join them.

"Joseph, you stay here with your sister. If this doesn't go well, you will have to help protect this home," Andrew whispered to the young boy.

Joseph bowed his head understanding. The men rode up to the verandah with an extra horse saddled. Andrew leaped upon the horse. He gazed back at Olivia, and then the small group of men took off on their horses leaving a cloud of dust.

"Joseph let's get started, get everything and everyone into the hidden room and tell Sadie to prepare the other women to be brought to the house. Let them sit in the living room, and then you go out and scout around the home. You are the guard, our lookout. Whistle the Catawba call if you see or hear anything."

"I will," the young boy said tightening his grip on his gun hanging in its holster, as he walked back down the steps of the verandah.

"Annie," Olivia yelled, rushing into the foyer. "You help Sadie with Benjamin and see that they have everything in the hidden room.

The minutes ticked by with anxiety overcoming Olivia. She couldn't have Andrew come home to her and then be taken away. Life couldn't be that unfair.

She set a rifle at the front and back door just in case. This time she wasn't going to be caught off guard remembering that smelly disgusting man grabbing her earlier in the day.

Olivia heard a whisper from the back of the house. Joseph silently pulled open the door hurrying inside. He closed it quietly.

"I saw two men lurking out back near the old barn. They must have snuck off from the others. I don't think that it's silver or gold they are looking for or at least not with the looks on their faces or what they were talking about."

Her body tightened as she indignantly grabbed the rifle. She understood very well what those men were after.

"You go get everyone into the hidden room. Stay there with them. Don't come out no matter what you hear."

"I will see to everyone, and get them settled, but I can't leave you."

"You have to stay with them in case I fail. They wouldn't be any match for those men. Do as I say, Joseph, hurry. I mean it don't come out no matter what you hear."

His head nodded okay, but his eyes were telling a different story.

Peeking out the back window, she gripped the rifle in her hand. She saw one of the men peeking out from behind the shed. She had a plan. She began humming as if she knew nothing about their presence. She pretended to work alone around the room, teasing the men.

The two men grinned, feeling like they had won. They came out of hiding.

She reached down holding onto the rifle, just as she had been taught by Cyrus, and raised it to the open window. She fired. The shot rang, echoing in her head.

One man grabbed his chest. Blood began gushing down his body. He started moaning and dropped to his knees. Then, he fell to the ground face forward becoming silent.

Understanding she had just killed a man, Olivia stood still with her arms trembling though, there was another enemy still out there. Her hands gripped her pistol, raised the gun up, and fired at the other man coming near the door. He fell to the ground with a loud thud with his haunting eyes looking up at her. She prepared her gun and rifle and listened to be sure there weren't any more men.

She heard a noise on the verandah. She ran to the front window, clutching the rifle wrapped in her arm.

"Olivia," yelled Andrew, "we heard shots!" He continued frantically to yell knocking on the door.

"Andrew," she called out unlocking and opening the front door. "I just shot two men out back." She stood there nervously tapping the rifle's butt on the wood floor.

"Yes, we heard the shots," he said grabbing the gun. "I could not account for two missing men from the regiment."

"The others?" she asked.

"Done," he declared, wrapping his arm around her trembling body. "But, Cyrus got shot."

"Is he…"

"No, he will be fine." He held onto her with her body quivering in his arms.

"Mister Andrew, is Miss Olivia alrights?" Big John hollered, bringing Cyrus into the house.

"Yes, John," Andrew called back, as the huge man stepped into the room. "She shot the other two men."

"They are out back by the old barn," Olivia replied, looking at Cyrus.

Big John nodded his head with a smile, "We gots 'em, Bella Oak is fines."

"Take him back to the cot in the back room," Olivia gasped seeing all of the blood on Cyrus.

Terrance came running into the house, "Here's your bag, Andrew."

I will see ter alls the men, Mr. Andrew," explained Big John looking over at Olivia.

"Good, John, take all of their weapons and anything valuable then, bring it back here. Bury those men leaving no trace. They can't ever be found."

"I will see to everything, Mr. Andrew. I shor' glad yous' is fine Miss Olivia and I'm proud of yo."

"Thank you Big John," Olivia said briskly walking into the office. "Oh, I better hurry and get everyone out."

"Out," Andrew yelled back at her, as he spun around following her to the office.

"Yes," she answered opening the bookcase letting the women step out with Joseph in the lead.

"Jane," Olivia grabbed the woman, "Cyrus has been shot but he is going to be fine. Come with me to the back room. Cyrus is in there," she said.

"Is it over," asked Joseph with an anxious face. "I heard gunshots."

"For now, son, but there will be more. Your sister shot two of the men." Andrew stood looking at the hidden room. "Everyone can go back home." His eyes were glued on the room.

"Father had Terrance and Benjamin build it so we could hide everything and everyone in it," Olivia answered seeing his curiosity.

"Then, William was worried."

"Yes, after you left, the stories of the war grew coming closer, so he had to have a place to keep everyone safe."

"A very wise man. I'm sorry," he said in a soft voice ducking his head down, "this was such a rough time and that I wasn't here to help keep you safe."

"You're here now and that is all that counts. You know you will be in trouble with the Union Army."

"Yes, and I might have to use that room if anyone comes looking for me. I have to see to Cyrus." He turned and raced to the back of the house.

There lying on the cot was Cyrus looking ill. Olivia's memories of her father in that room made her uneasy.

"His wound wasn't deep; it went into this shoulder. I've already checked the wound. I just have to clean it some more and stitch it up." Andrew quickly began pulling out instruments from his bag.

Cyrus lay there looking up at him with Jane standing to his side.

"Relax, Cyrus."

Andrew placed the cloth on the old man's face and he closed his eyes. Olivia stood watching Andrew easily clean and stitch the wound.

"There, he will be better soon. Jane, you and Mama Bea watch him. He will just have to rest for a few days. Good food and rest is the best medicine."

"It shor' is nice to have a doctor around the house," Olivia declared proudly.

He smiled down on her leading her out of the room.

"Come on," she began, "you can change into some other clothes, we can't have you walking around dressed in a Yankee uniform," she said grabbing his arm. "Benjamin's and Father's clothes are upstairs. Some of them should fit and then we are burning that uniform."

"I guess I will become a true Southerner, then."

She nodded an approving head. A smile emerged. She took his arm going up the stairs into her parents' bedroom.

He went to the armoire finding some clothes that would work. He looked around the massive room. "Your mother hasn't changed anything; it's the same as when I was here last."

"Yes, it is too difficult on her," she stammered holding back tears, seeing all of her father's personal items.

"I understand."

He pulled her to him. She let go of him and turned back around wiping her face.

Andrew picked out some clothing and began to dress. He took his shirt off and she could see the scar on his side from his gunshot wound. She shuddered staring at the zigzagged stitches knowing how close she had come to losing him.

"Olivia, I'm fine," he said, feeling the scare as he buttoned up his shirt. "Stop worrying." When he finished dressing, he turned around, "How do I look?"

Olivia laughed. "Now, you look like a Southern gentlemen but jest don't talk." She picked up his dirty Union uniform.

"I figure I will learn to drawl *jest* like you, in time," he added trying out his Southern accent.

"Not yet." She reached up to him. "You, my love, will always be my Northern gentlemen and that is fine with me."

"Olivia," Annie called out from the bottom of the staircase, "supper is ready."

"Wow, time shor' has flown," he said laughing.

She smiled at him.

"Let's go eat. I'm hungry," he added leading her out of her mother and father's bedroom.

Andrew sat down at the table. His body was erect with confidence. His head tilted and a smile came on his face listening to talk and laughter emerging from the table. He was now home and all was well for the time being.

When supper ended, he slipped his arm in Olivia's arm leading her to the office. He twirled her around facing him.

"My dear, now that I am home, I do have to keep my promise," he added smiling.

"You shor' do. Andrew Robert Drake, a gentlemen always keeps his promise."

He leaned in hugging her, "Well, is there a preacher nearby? I do have my honor and I must make an honest woman of you."

"I reckon you better," she said chuckling. "I can get a preacher to come out to Bella Oak, but we haven't set a date."

"Well girl, get to planning."

"Let me see. How about Sunday the eighteenth? How does that sound?"

"Perfect."

"Now you can't back out! We have a date set."

"Yes," he added pulling her close.

"Andrew, your eyes are telling me something."

"Yes, that I'm a man in love."

"I'm afraid more than that. You haven't had any sleep, have you?"

"No, but I don't want to miss one second with you."

"We have the rest of our lives to be together. Having you home is enough for now. You need rest."

This time she wasn't taking no for an answer as she led him up the stairs.

"Ah, I see I have to stay in the guest bedroom alone."

"Andrew Drake, where's that Northern gentleman."

"He's gone," he said winking.

"You get some rest. We will be fine. Big John and the others will take turns guarding the plantation. So you don't have anything to worry about." She leaned in kissing him goodnight.

"I swanny, it's difficult to let you go," he added with a Southern drawl. He laughed, with his hands rubbing her back.

"Get some sleep and goodnight, my love."

"Goodnight, Olivia," he whispered, leaving the door open so he could hear any slight disturbance. He never appreciated a real bed with real sheets so much. He quickly fell to sleep.

Olivia went back downstairs to check on Cyrus. He was asleep. Then she went to her bedroom where Annie was reading.

"Your dream has come true. I am so happy for you," she offered. "Maybe there is hope for me, too so then, we'll both get our Southern dreams."

Olivia looked at her young sister. She sure wasn't the same naïve girl of a couple of summers ago. This war had taken the innocence away from everyone.

Olivia bowed her head, "Oh Annie, we are going to make it. I have to believe that. I close my eyes and think that Andrew's being home is a dream and he will vanish right in front of me."

"Olivia, pushaw! He is real."

"Then, Miss Annie Bellamead, we have to plan my wedding for the eighteenth."

"Yes!" She jumped up laying the book down on the bed. "Mother, are we bringing her home?" she questioned getting excited. Olivia could see the young sweet girl was emerging.

"No, she is better off in Charleston, for now. Don't look so sad. I'm having a small wedding, so don't start going overboard with planning."

"Olivia, I'm sorry, Father and Mother," she became quiet, "and Benjamin won't be here."

"Andrew is here and that is all the wedding that I need. I am going to wear Mother's wedding dress, and Joseph can give me away. And you…you can be my Maid of Honor, perfect!"

"There are some pretty wild flowers out back," Annie added, "Mama Bea and I can make you a pretty nosegay bouquet to carry."

"Yes, and I will have to send a message to the preacher, but we can't let the town know about Andrew. We can't let folks around here find out he is living with us, not until the war is over. It's jest too dangerous."

"Everything will work, you jest wait and see," Annie exclaimed falling back into her bed. "Oh, you won't be my roommate anymore," she laughed, sighing and giggling.

"No, I won't, but it won't be long and you will be getting married yourself young lady."

"I hope the war will be over then."

"I pray it will be. We will have the best wedding for you, Annie. You are and will always be Bella Oak's true Southern belle."

"But, Olivia, you are Bella Oak's defender and a Southern belle."

"No, Benjamin was and he will always be Bella Oak's defender and I, my sweet sister, am not a Southern belle, but I am a Southern girl. I better go check on Andrew. He was so tired. I hope he is asleep," she said softly getting out of her bed.

She peeked into the silent room with the sounds of a quiet snore softly flowing. She closed the door, leaning against it and whispered, "He is real."

Chapter Twenty-Five
"The Yankees are Coming"

On Wednesday, October fourteenth, the sun was radiating into the room through the old oak flickering across Olivia's bed. She had slept soundly for the first time in months. Andrew was near and all was well. With her nightclothes slipped off, she put her dress on. She combed her long hair pulling it back away from her face into a twist. She stopped by Andrew's closed door and could hear the quiet snore continuing. A smile came across her face. This was just the medicine for him, to be safe at home.

Annie was already up and seeing to things down in the dining room. She was learning to handle the plantation.

"Good morning, sleepy head," Annie chuckled, picking up the plates on the dining room table.

"Good morning, Annie and thank you for seeing to everyone," she said holding onto the back of a dining room chair.

"You're welcome, I'm glad you and Andrew rested. I'm pleased he is still sleeping. We can't have a tired bride and groom."

"I did sleep better than I have in a long time."

"Sit down and I will get you some food. Mama Bea made grits and biscuits; we still have a little flour left. I'm shor' glad your night was filled with nice dreams and not bad ones like they have been."

Annie came back into the room and placed a plate in front of Olivia.

"Yes, my dreams are coming true."

"Good," came, a voice behind her.

"Andrew," she twirled around in her chair, "good morning! You look better."

"I feel better. It is a good morning," he leaned over kissing her on the forehead. "Are you just getting up, too?"

"Yes, I caught up on some much needed rest as well."

"Sit down and have some breakfast," Annie urged, smiling taking her job of seeing to everyone seriously.

"Yes, Ma'am," he replied sitting down in his chair at the head of the table. "The day is so gorgeous. I'm going to check out the plantation and Big John said he would help me and show me around."

"Well, I have some work in the garden and I'll check the food that we have hidden and see how we are doing."

He took the last bite of his biscuit.

"Annie, thank you for breakfast." He slid his chair back from the table. "My dear, I will see you later. Oh that sounds so nice." He leaned over putting his arms around her.

"Yes, it does." She stood, smiled, and turned to leave the room.

Annie was working inside and Olivia was in the garden when she heard Terrance shouting. She ran around to the verandah with Andrew and Big John coming from the barn.

"The Yankees are coming," he screamed with terror in his face.

"What?" Andrew shouted, running up to him.

"I saw a large troop of Union soldiers marching this way. They are carrying the Union flag and the commanders are riding in the front. Andrew, there are hundreds not a small militia."

"Go tell Cyrus. John, you stay in the barn and Jonas you go home with the women, Terrance, you and Joseph hide out on the plantation. You, my dear, and I will hide out in the house. If there is a commander, they may be moving on. I hope they don't decide to use Bella Oak as their headquarters."

"No, I will kill them first," Olivia screamed.

"Now Olivia, stay calm. It will be your job to convince them the other Union soldiers aren't around. They are the reason the troop is here."

She nodded her head turning to go back into the home. The day had been so perfect.

"Let's get prepared," she ordered, stomping back into the house. "More Yankees."

Everyone stood ready. Andrew told them to make the plantation look normal, leaving the women to stay out working, all except Annie. He wanted to keep her safe in the hidden room.

"Olivia, I have to stay hidden. Like you said, my Southern accent isn't perfected yet and someone might recognize me." He smiled giving her a kiss trying to calm her. "I will stand here ready to help, but if they come inside I will hide in the room with Annie."

Her body tensed. The war was too close, and the opposition was on Bella Oak coming up to the house.

"Can you handle this?" Andrew asked looking at her distressed face.

"Yes, I will handle them jest fine," she announced with a determined voice as her face grew stern. She grabbed a shawl putting it around her shoulders picked up her pistol hiding it underneath.

The noise of the troops marching near, pounding onto the ground was thumping in her head. There were so many. She looked out the window and they trampled the once beautiful fields coming close to the home.

"That is Major General Quincy Gillmore," Andrew whispered, "his orders were to take Fort Sumter and Charleston. I have heard he is a fair man."

Her body froze. That was the commander that had led the fight against General Beauregard and her father. He was the commander that killed Benjamin in Charleston. How could she face that man? Then, she looked over at Andrew and knew why she must face the commander. She wouldn't risk Andrew's life for revenge.

Her hand trembled gripping the knob pushing the door open with a squeak. She moved out to the center of the verandah. Many of the men hooted and jeered, and the commander held up his hand to silence them. The massive group of men on horses in front of her was overpowering. Even the creaking of the leather saddles as the men repositioned themselves to halt the horses was unnerving.

She stood gripping her hidden pistol ready to fire. She knew that she could take down the commander first and go down fighting if she had to. She said a silent prayer with her eyes fixed on the men lined up as far as she could see.

Many faces were worn and distressed, but the soldiers were ready to fight and kill to preserve the Union. It helped to remember how Andrew described the men at night, all little boys needing someone to assure them of morning coming. She took a deep breath staring at the commander as he towered on his strong steed in front of her next to the steps of Bella Oak.

"Ma'am," the man jumped down from his horse, stepping up onto the verandah. He wasn't so overwhelming face to face. He was a short man with graying hair, tired eyes, and a strained face. "I don't wish to cause you any harm, but I am looking for a small militia of my men. Have you seen them?"

"Sir, there ain't any Yankees on Bella Oak."

"Ma'am, are you here alone?"

"No, Sir, I have my slaves who have stayed."

"I see. Then, you won't mind my searching for them on your property?"

"I don't tell falsehoods, Sir. There are no Yankees here, but you may come in, only you." She stepped back still staring at all of the men in front of the plantation home. She smiled to herself the only Yankees that were on the plantation were buried and Andrew didn't count, so she wasn't lying.

The man stepped up next to her looking down sympathetically at her. She wondered if maybe he was thinking of his own daughter or wife being left with the Rebel soldiers coming in on them. She held the door and he marched into the foyer with authority looking around at the grand home. He knew his men's mission was to destroy this grand plantation. Olivia gazed into the man's eyes as he scrutinized everything. His lips curled into a small smile taking everything into account about the grand home.

"May I," he asked, waving his arm towards the office. He walked as his boots hammered on the hard wood floors.

"Yes." She held her breath as they entered and prayed that the secret room would stay hidden from his eyes.

He peered around the room, turned, and walked out the door. She followed him to the back of the home. She breathed a sigh of relief knowing Andrew was safe for now.

"This cot has blood on it," Gillmore questioned with his eyes narrowing, holding tight to his pistol hanging on his side.

Mama Bea was standing back in the corner of the room with her black eyes watching the Yankees every move. Sadie stood next to Mama Bea holding tight to Benjamin.

"Cyrus, our foreman, had an accident out with the cattle the other day and was brought here for me to see to him."

He seemed to believe her story and continued checking out the dining room and parlor. He stood back in the foyer, peering up the staircase. He waved his arm for her to go first and he followed her up the long stairs. She stepped as her mother had taught as any fine Southern belle would, slowly making her way to the top. He held onto his hat stepping up the stairs behind her. She could hear his sword clank next to his pistol. Her heart pounded. She was still holding onto her pistol. This man had kind eyes, but wouldn't hesitate to shoot her.

He went from room to room. She smiled. Andrew, Mama Bea, or Sadie had made the beds, not leaving any trace of someone else sleeping there.

He turned around following her down the stairs. "Well, my lady, I shall have my men check out the rest of this fine plantation, if you don't mind?"

"Sir, you are the only Yankees on Bella Oak," she asserted as worry came over her wondering if he was going to finish his mission of destroying the massive plantation home.

She remembered her father's commenting about the Yankees burning property. This couldn't happen, not now. She stood on the porch and watched the men search the barns and fields.

When they were finished, Gillmore stepped up next to her on the verandah with his hat in his hand.

"My fight isn't with the women of the South. Good day, my lady."

He gave her a smile, not letting his troops see. He was leaving Bella Oak to stand for another day. He put his hat back on but looked at her with suspicious eyes. He walked up to his strong horse and put his boot into the stirrup hoisting his body into his saddle. He dipped his head.

This may be war, but Major General Gillmore did have some decency about him. He knew his men's intentions, those who he had sent ahead on the scouting mission, weren't on the behalf of the war. He turned his horse around and all of the troops followed him as they all stared back for a final look at her. She didn't move until all of the Yankees were off Bella Oak.

Andrew and Annie came out from the hidden room and stood out of sight in the doorway. Terrance ran up to the verandah and into the foyer. He had been hiding out watching from the old oak on the other side of the spring creek.

"Andrew, yous' need to stay hidden fur a while. He might leave a few men waitin' and watchin' 'round Bella Oak."

"Yes, I'm afraid you're right," Andrew answered sighing. "You, my dear, Olivia," pulling her close, "put on a sterling act."

"I was so worried he would find you and burn Bella Oak," she said in a low voice so nervously. "He seemed to know what I had done, but he didn't do anything."

"The commanders on both sides have seen enough bloodshed and destruction. Most don't desire to see more without cause."

"I'm glad we hid all of their swords and weapons in the hidden room. What is it, Andrew," Olivia questioned. "Are we safe now, or not?"

"Not! If this many Union soldiers are here, then the Rebels are being pushed back. The battles are getting closer."

"Mr. Andrew," called out John hurrying from the backside of the home.

"What is it, John?"

"Those Yankees tooks all de cattles and most chickens weez had left. They did leaves one ol' cow fur milkin', I guess fur the little boy and we has a fews chickens."

Olivia's face grew stern with her hands gripping making fists.

"Calm down," Andrew grabbed her hands, "you still have Bella Oak."

"Yes, but those damn Yankees! We're getting low on food." She paused for a moment then continued, "We have to be on guard and stay near the house."

She wrapped her arm around Andrew, holding him tight.

"Now it's time to prepare lunch with what food we have left," she said. "Let's go count our blessings and eat."

That afternoon, she sent a message to the preacher and he returned his message thrilled about the good news. He promised that he would keep her secret. It was settled, the wedding would take place on Sunday.

That evening after supper, she walked into the office and fell into one of the big leather chairs. It had been a long tiring day and she wasn't able to get the picture out of her mind of all of those Yankee soldiers covering Bella Oak in a wave of blue.

Andrew was building a fire and she noticed the drapes were pulled, another sign of war to hide him in case the Yankees were watching. The room began to warm. She moved onto the floor next to him. He poked the fire and sparks flew. She could see the worry on his face in the light of the flames. Their carefree morning had vanished with the Yankees' arrival.

"It's going to storm tonight. I hear it thundering and the wind is picking up," she whispered softly. She leaned back with her hands on the floor behind her.

"Yes, just as it did the night that summer before I left." His eyes stared off into the fire, hiding his thoughts from her.

She reached up touching his face turning it towards her. She wasn't able to hide her own emotions.

"Andrew," she whispered with her voice trailing off.

He stared into those green eyes, "With me here, I'm putting you in danger."

"With your not being here, I'm in danger. So, don't even think about leaving," she corrected. She pulled him close as their lips squeezed together.

Her insides were warm with emotions stirring and she couldn't or wouldn't deny her feeling. She snuggled next to him as their thoughts of the Yankees disappeared. It was just as it was the day of the picnic. She wasn't worried about acting like a lady and social graces were gone. She wasn't stopping. Neither of them worried about the rest of the world.

He softly moved her long thick hair from her face revealing her eyes As he glided his hand down her back, her body throbbed with passion. Her eyes closed with her hand touching his chest as he pulled her closer. Their passion taking over and their bodies intertwined as their love became free for a fleeting moment.

They lay there in the peaceful silence with their bodies caressing in front of the hearth and the light of the fire flickering on their faces, neither leaving the room tonight. This is where they were staying. She was his and he was hers for the night cuddling next to each other, not having to speak. Their bodies did the talking with the thunder echoing like cannons firing, reminding them of the war and how short life could be.

The room began to cool as the fire burned out. They woke to a new day. She could see the worry on Andrew's face as he stood by the window peering out.

"No, you aren't leaving. You are staying right here," she assured, understanding what was on his mind. "I can't have anyone else leave Bella Oak. It will devastate me, and we will keep you safe. They believe you are dead along with the others. Promise me you will stay forever and never leave."

He turned back around with his eyes sparkling, "I promise, you know that you always get your way."

"Well, I have and I don't intend to stop just because of this war. Now, there is work to be done around here."

She walked over to the desk picking up her father's writing paper.

"You, sir, can't put off sending your father a letter explaining what has happened. Tell him to stay quiet when they tell him of your death. I will address the envelope for you in my name in case someone is spying..."

"Yes," Andrew interrupted, stating sadly, "instead of my being deceased, he will hear of his old friend's demise, not much of a trade."

"My father's death may make him sad, but your death would destroy him. Tell him the happy news. Tell him about our wedding, a little brightness in the sorrow."

He pulled back the drapes and stared out to the old oak tree across the creek.

"It's still a beauty isn't it?" she offered holding onto his arm.

"I won't ever forget climbing up into the old tree seeing the countryside so far away. I hope someday to climb back up there when all this is over."

"We both will… Dreams do come true here on Bella Oak."

"Yes, my little Southern dream, they do."

"Now, let's have some breakfast, I'm starving," she grinned, grabbing his arm and pulling him toward the door.

They sat down at the table. Annie had to bite her lip as she looked at her sister's wrinkled clothes. She knew Olivia had not come to bed the night before. The only action that could have made Annie happier is if she had been the one missing from the bedroom with her true love.

Chapter Twenty-Six
"Olivia's New Life"

Sunday, October eighteenth arrived and Olivia was standing in her parent's bedroom looking in the mirror. Mama Bea and Annie had helped her dress and helped her arrange her hair.

Tears grew in Mama Bea's eyes. "Yous' is beautiful, child, jest likes yo' mother so longs ago. Yo' Father would has love ter be here," she said shaking her head, believing this wasn't right.

"Mama Bea...Father and Benjamin are here." She hugged the old woman. "Now we have a wedding to get started.

Annie and Mama Bea went down the stairs first, Annie to play the piano and Mama Bea to add final details to the wedding cake. Joseph met Olivia at the top of the stairs and looped his arm inside hers. They stepped down the steps slowly when they heard Annie playing the wedding march.

Olivia could see Andrew standing in the parlor. She remembered walking down the stairs holding onto Benjamin before he left for Charleston to warn their father. She smiled feeling his presents. Annie stopped playing the piano and moved in beside Olivia. They all stood in the parlor listening to the preacher began to speak.

"My friends, we are gathered here to join this man and this woman." The words continued with Olivia looking into Andrew's eyes. Her dream was becoming a reality. The preacher pronounced them husband and wife and they kissed. She was now Mrs. Andrew Robert Drake.

Jonas, Terrance, and Cyrus gave her hugs and Big John stood there fidgeting as she walked up and hugged him too. This was her family. All the women were sniffling, and little Benjamin was jabbering as Sadie smiled at the bride holding him close. Mama Bea stood over to the side with tears running down her face. Olivia wrapped her arms around her as the woman took her in her arms just as she had done when she was a little girl.

"Well Andrew," Joseph admitted, "you are now a plantation owner. That is a lot of responsibility, but if you can handle Olivia, then you won't have any problems taking care of this plantation," he said laughing.

The celebration continued with Annie playing the piano. Andrew took Olivia in his arms and they danced in the parlor. It wasn't like twirling around on the dance floor at the picnic, but this time, they were finally husband and wife.

Everyone danced, sang, and ate, having a great time. Bella Oak came alive for one day and once more they all forgot about the war and the hard times.

Months move on and rumors of the battles continued. Food had become scarce and the lone cow didn't produce enough milk. It seemed the other plantations were like Bella Oak; the Yankees had cleaned them out as well.

The news of the Yankees raiding the Dawson's plantation and burning it came right before Christmas. The once magnificent home now was standing as a shell with its outside walls the only reminder of its former home. The realization of how close Bella

Oak had come to being destroyed was haunting. That dreadful day, the Dawson family hid in their cellar, knowing the Yankees would love to finish their job, shooting Lawrence.

Olivia knew that Andrew had saved them by warning them of the militia. The raiders were stealing from the plantations and leaving a trail of killing and rape. She still was in awe that the Yankees had not cleaned her home out the day that General Gillmore searched Bella Oak. She still wondered why he didn't let his men steal and destroy the home.

The Montgomery plantation had been raided. They lost everything, but the home was left standing and the family was safe.

Big John fished from the river and ponds each day. He brought home plenty of fish to fry, so along with the canned vegetables from the summer, they were all right for the time being. Coffee and sugar were a luxury that they had to do without.

One cool day in December, Olivia heard a ruckus in the parlor. She rushed into the room and there standing grinning was Terrance and Joseph with a Christmas tree in front of the window.

"Benjamin has to have a tree," Joseph beamed.

"Yes, he does," Olivia agreed.

She and Annie began to add the decorations that Joseph brought down from the attic. They turned the parlor into a delightful Christmas scene.

Christmas morning, they excitedly watched as the tiny boy as quickly as his short legs would take him to the tall tree. He grinned and squealed looking at the presents. Jonas carved him a horse and cow and Annie knitted him a sweater. They didn't have a lot to eat, but they did have Christmas that year and everyone sang carols along with Big John leading them in song after song. All of them spent the day telling wonderful Christmas stories from the past.

The New Year 1864 came in with Andrew kissing Olivia at midnight in their bedroom. "This is our new life, a new year," he assured smiling down on her.

Cyrus, a few weeks later, was standing on the verandah holding onto his hat turning it around in his hands nervously. "Olivia, I'm sorry, but Jane and I are leaving."

"Cyrus, why?" she called out anxiously.

"This has been too much on her with me getting shot and the Yankees coming onto Bell Oak. She would like to move into town with her family. She believes we will be safer."

"I see." She stared at the older man as he ducked his head down.

"I'm sorry to leave; your father treated me so well, but this is what I have to do."

"I understand," she said stepping up to him. "I'm going to miss you." She looked at the man who had helped build Bella Oak.

"I will be back to visit and after the war, I would like a chance to come back."

"You will always be welcome here. This is your home. Cyrus, when are you leaving?"

"This afternoon."

"Well, I guess this is goodbye," she assured reaching out to the man that had taught her to ride a horse and shoot a gun. He had been right there her entire life.

"I said my goodbyes to Joseph. He has growed to become a fine young man."

He turned back around stepping off the verandah. He put his hat back on with his head still bent down.

It seemed Cyrus wasn't going to be the only one to leave Bella Oak. Ruth had insisted that Annie and Joseph come to visit.

"Olivia, I'm staying and help you with Bella Oak, I can't leave," Joseph concluded. "With Cyrus leaving and Big John taking Annie to Charleston that makes you low on men."

"We will be fine," Andrew added patting the young man on the back. "Look, you don't have to stay long, maybe having Annie there will be enough for mother and you will be able to come back home with Big John."

"Then I will go see mother, get Annie settled, and be back shortly," Joseph agreed.

"You should be going with us, Olivia," Annie declared. "My absence will be too much work on you."

"My life is here with Andrew and Bella Oak. You tell Mother I love her and give her a hug for me. I just hope she is doing alright."

"Her letters seem like she is back to her normal self," Annie replied looking at her older sister. "Oh, it is so difficult to leave."

"Yes, it is," Olivia answered, hugging Annie. She stood there holding onto her siblings. She now would be the only Bellamead left at Bella Oak.

Joseph still protested a little, but climbed up into the buggy that January twenty-fifth with Big John and Annie.

"I will be home soon," he called out with the horse's hoofs clipping on the rocks and the buggy heading down the path and out the gates.

Olivia stood with tears running down her face. Andrew pulled her close. He could hear sobs coming from the inside of the home. She had asked Mama Bea to go with them, but she refused. This was her home and she had Olivia to take care of. Ruth and Violia had others who would see to Joseph and Annie.

A few weeks later, the sun was beginning to warm the ground and it was time to plant the seeds in the garden. Olivia was outside with Sadie.

Suddenly, Olivia saw the sky began to spin, and she fell to the ground. Sadie screamed. Andrew and Terrance ran from the barn. Andrew lifted her up, took her in the house, and laid her on the cot in the back room. She opened her eyes looking at him.

"What happened?" she question looking at his eyes and Mama Bea and Sadie standing over her.

He grinned, "Well it seems we will be having a guest by the end of summer," he announced.

"What?" she asked sitting up, "no, it can't be. You shor'?"

"Yes, I am a doctor, my dear."

Olivia fell back on the cot. Mama Bea grinned and laughed with joy as she walked back to the kitchen.

Now, Olivia's life would be fulfilled. A baby!

Chapter Twenty-Seven
"Jonas"

The warm summer came in with a vengeance full of heat, blistering hot. Terrance, Jonas, and Andrew kept things going on the plantation and Sadie helped Olivia with the garden.

One smothering morning, Monday, July eighteenth, Olivia was in the barn milking the cow. She heard horses riding up. She hurried to the barn door believing it was Andrew, but something stopped her before she stepped outside. A wisp of air hit the back of her neck and then a voice from behind her called out, "Shoot them."

She cautiously peered out the door. There standing in front of the home were four men, scalawags, two dressed in old Union uniforms, laughing and carrying on. She took a deep breath. She was alone and only Jonas was on the plantation to help.

Andrew had gone into town, Dr. Holt had been hurt and Andrew was called to see to him. Terrance was riding out to the

Montgomery plantation to buy some baby chicks that had recently hatched.

She saw Jonas coming out of his home not noticing the men. He stopped, they fired, and he fell to the ground. Sadie screamed. Benjamin came walking out onto the verandah and one of the men laughed and aimed his gun at him. Olivia pulled her rifle up and fired knocking the man off his horse. He fell to the ground with a loud thud. Another man fired at her. She ducked into the barn reloading her rifle. She fired back hitting him. She reloaded the rifle once more and prepared to fire. It jammed. The other two angry men leaped off their horses running at the barn. She pulled out her pistol and shot one but knew she couldn't reload to shoot the other man. He stood a few feet from her and grinned. Suddenly his eyes grew wide and he fell face-down lying in front of her. Jonas stood to the side with blood running down his chest. He dropped his gun as his body slipped to the ground. Sadie ran to him.

She heard horses riding up. She picked up her pistol, but saw that it was Terrance and Andrew. They ran to Jonas seeing the four dead men.

Annella screamed, "Jonas, Jonas!" She rushed across the yard falling down on her knees next to her husband.

"Mamma!" Terrance shouted out hurrying over to his father.

Sadie grabbed the old woman.

Terrance reached under the old man's shoulders and Andrew grabbed his legs. Jonas looked up at Terrance, "Is everyones alrights?"

"Yes father, you saved them," Terrance replied with his voice breaking up.

They laid him on the cot in the back room. Andrew pulled the round ball out of Jonas's chest. Terrance stood looking down at his father, watching while Andrew stitched him up.

Andrew's face was grim. He shook his head looking up at Terrance. "It's not good" Andrew said as he pulled himself up.

"He saved us," Olivia offered overwhelmed. "My rifle jammed and the men were coming at me. I was so terrified. I wasn't able to kill the last man. Their faces were so angry. None of us would have lived had it not been for Jonas."

"Terrance," Sadie added with tears running down her face. "they wuz going ter shoot Benjamin," she softly whispered holding tight to her son. "But…Miss Olivia shots the mens."

"I'm so sorry I wasn't here," Terrance cried out grabbing Sadie. He realized that he almost lost his entire family.

Annella squatted down by Jonas lying still on the cot. Her head leaned next to his face with tears falling off her tired cheek.

Andrew's eyes were brimming with tears as he stood looking down at the man who had saved his wife and unborn baby. He wrapped his arm around Olivia holding her tight.

Jonas opened his eyes. "Son I's got those mens. Dey wuz going to hurt de little Ben and Miss Olivia."

"Father, you saved everyone here."

"I loves yous' and that boy. Takes care of him," he whispered as he gulped for air.

"I will father," Terrance said. He bent down touching his father's face.

Don'ts cries so. Yous' has de boy to sees to. I loves yo'," his body relaxed and Andrew bent down.

"He's gone," he said closing Jonas's eyes. Annella continued to sob uncontrollably and Terrance held her by her shoulders. Sadie stood shaking, and Benjamin cried, scared.

Andrew led Olivia out of the room to leave the family alone. He stood in the office looking out the window.

"Why?" he questioned.

"I don't know," she whispered moving close seeing the dead men lying everywhere.

"I have some graves to dig," he said overwhelmed, leaning down kissing her. "You stay here and rest."

A little while later Terrance came into the room. "Where's Andrew?"

"He's gone to see to the dead men. Terrance, I'm so sorry…I tried…" she sobbed.

"Olivia, yo' and my father saved my wife and son. Don't be sorry."

She heard his boots clicking on the wood floor as he stepped outside. She could see out the window, the look on his face staring down on the coarse men that had killed his father.

The small group once more stood in the cemetery saying goodbye to Jonas, another loved one killed by the war. Andrew read from the *Bible* and said a prayer as they all sang *Amazing Grace*, this time without Big John.

Sadie placed some flowers on grave she'd picked by the verandah. Some of Ruth's prized flowers were still growing through the weeds even without the tender care that they were used to.

Olivia smiled looking down at the beautiful flowers. Bella Oak was like them and would survive through this war just as the flowers.

Andrew, Olivia, and Mama Bea moved under the shade of a large old oak to give the family some time alone. Then, Olivia walked to her father's grave.

"Father, it is another sad day on Bella Oak. You see to Jonas, he saved my life and your grandchild's. Benjamin, thank you for saving me, just as you tried to save father. My dear brother, I know you are still looking after me."

Andrew's face scrunched not understanding what she was saying. He looked over at Mama Bea, but she was nodding her head affirmatively.

"I was going to walk out of the barn," she began, "believing it was you riding up, Andrew, but I heard a whisper that commanded, 'shoot them.' I stopped before I made it to the door and grabbed my rifle. It was Benjamin's voice; I would know his voice anywhere."

"Thank you, my young friend," Andrew whispered peering down at Benjamin's grave.

"No," she smiled back at Andrew, "your brother."

"Yes, my brother," Andrew said proudly, curling his arm around her tight.

"Now, my dear, it's time for you to go back to the house and rest," Andrew said as he led her to the buggy and helped her climb in.

Chapter Twenty-Eight
"Mary Ruth"

The plantation was quiet, too quiet. Terrance's heart was broken, losing his father not long after losing Benjamin, his best friend. This war had caused too many deaths.

Big John and Joseph had planned to stay a while with Ruth, Violia, and Annie. However, after receiving word of Jonas's death, the men would be coming home as soon as possible.

It was Tuesday, August twenty-ninth. Andrew was out back chopping wood for the cook stove. Olivia was sitting in the parlor knitting a baby gown, preparing for the new arrival. She stood and pain shot through her body. She hollered for Mama Bea, and she came running.

"I's goin' and gets Mr. Andrew," Mama Bea said as she smiled at the young girl.

Olivia could hear her long dress swishing back and forth hurrying down the hallway. Andrew came running into the room drenched in sweat.

"Here," he said putting his wet arm around her. "This child is going to be like you, with a mind of its own, not waiting for the coolness of evening."

He carefully helped her up the stairs.

He prepared and cleaned his hands and arms as Mama Bea helped her into the bed. Seeing Olivia's eyes wild with fear, Mama Bea smiled down on her and held her hand. The time moved on slowly, and it turned into hours. She lay there in the warm room with what breeze there was from the window. This day was smothering hot.

"I knew it, this baby is so like you, making us wait in this heat," Andrew teased anxiously.

She let out a cry of pain and Andrew prepared to deliver his child. Here he was a great surgeon, but was so nervous. Then his skilled hands lifted up his baby girl.

"I was right, she is just like you," he laughed laying the crying, green-eyed baby with soft curly hair in Olivia's arms.

"Mama Bea, why are you crying?"

"I remembers, de day, yo' father held yo' right here in this same room. He wuz so proud.

"Well come see our Mary Ruth," Olivia said playing with the tiny babies fingers. "Mary for Andrew's mother and Ruth for mine."

"She's beautiful jest as her mother," the old woman said overwhelmed, softly touching the baby's wild, curly hair. "Lets me cleans her ups," Mama Bea said lifting the soft bundle up into her old hands that had held many babies.

Andrew stared at his two girls.

"Everything is alright?" questioned Olivia, worriedly.

"Oh, yes," Andrew moved over to her, "I was just thinking about our fathers. I wish they were both here." He sat down on the bed by her.

"Well, as soon as this war is over, we will take Mary and go see your father," she added smiling up at him.

"Now," he chuckled, "we need to have a boy."

She shook his arm. "You jest give it a while," she assured grinning back at him.

Mama Bea walked back over with Mary, all cleaned up and dressed in her finery, handing her to Andrew.

"This is a wonderful day fur Bella Oak and another proud generation."

"Yes, it is Mama Bea. Life does continue on even with all of the pain and anguish. If Mary has half of the gumption of Olivia, then Bella Oak will continue," Andrew added smiling down on his sweet baby. "I pray she will have a tranquil, glorious, and prosperous life."

"Oh, I will have to continue my journal that I started when I was young. I would like her to know about her Uncle Benjamin, since he is around to protect her," Olivia grinned looking up at Mama Bea's reaction. "I have so much to add, mostly sad, but a lot of good."

Mary was a healthy and strong baby. A Bellamead would be nothing less. Olivia was sitting in the parlor as the baby nursed. Hearing a buggy roll up, she slid her breast inside her dress fastening it. She lifted Mary up seeing first who was outside.

Her heart pounded, "Mary, we have a guest."

She opened the door and there in front of her was her brother. Joseph jumped down from the buggy and leaped up onto the verandah.

"I'm home and I'm not leaving," he called out looking down on his sister and new niece.

He reached in giving Olivia a kiss on the cheek. Then he stopped.

"Awe, she is a spitting image of you. Father would be proud, she is a true Bellamead.

I guess with a little Drake in her." Andrew added. He stepped up and they shook hands then hugged.

"It's nice to have you home," Andrew spoke looking down at his small family.

"John, come see Mary Ruth."

The big man stepped up on the verandah clinching his hat in his hands nervously looking down at the tiny bundle Olivia was holding.

"She's shor' little bitties," he said with a grin on his face, "but's she is a beautiful angel."

Andrew turned and shook the big man's hand.

"Welcome home, John."

The screen door squeaked and Terrance stood silently.

"Terrance," Joseph voice became solemn, "I'm sorry about Jonas."

"Sos am I," Big John added, ducking down his head playing with his hat. "He wuz a good man."

"Yes, an he died bein' a good man," Terrance added with a hint of a smile on his face. "He saved this tiny precious baby."

"I sees der is a lot of works ter do around here," Big John added. He looked over at Olivia and smiled, proud he was home.

"Yes, there is. It has been a lot of work for Terrance and me," Andrew assured leaning in kissing his daughter.

"Let me change clothes," Joseph exclaimed happy to be home.

Joseph held the door. Olivia walked inside holding Mary in her arms.

"Now tell me about this Charleston girl."

"Annie," he squeezed his mouth with his lips curling into a smile.

"Yep, she has told me everything. You know she learned to be a spy with me and Jackson and she has become better at it now." Olivia added laughing laying Mary in her cradle.

"Her name is Madeline, but she isn't part of the right social group and Aunt Violia and mother don't approve, but Annie helped me spend time with her."

"Yes, Annie is a romantic at heart and she has missed Vincent," reported Olivia.

"You haven't heard?" Joseph asked.

Andrew alertly asked, "Heard what?"

"General Sherman's army has captured Atlanta, and Vincent and a few other boys have joined to fight for the South. I am going soon, a few more months."

"No, you're not," Olivia stomped her foot. "You are staying right here, we aren't losing another Bellamead to this war."

Joseph didn't say anything back.

"Oh, Annie…she didn't tell me," Olivia admitted worriedly.

"She received the letter from Vincent, addressed in my name so Mother wouldn't know, the day before we left."

I will have to send her a letter," Olivia sighed.

"My goodness, yo' has shor' growed," Mama Bea shouted, hurrying over to Joseph.

"Mama Bea, I haven't been gone that long, but I shor did miss you," Joseph said as he grabbed the large woman.

"I glad's yo' home," she insisted not able to let go.

"I better get changed. There is plenty of work to get done."

The young boy turned to go up the stairs, now looking like a man more than a boy.

Andrew leaned down kissing Olivia, "Things with him will be fine. I will see to that."

The news of Vincent was too hard on Annie and she had to come home. The first of October, she arrived, running up the steps of the verandah. Olivia handed her Mary and Annie beamed holding gently her niece, however Annie couldn't contain her tears; they began running down her face.

"Annie, are you alright?"

She bowed her head trying to conceal her anguish, "Your dream did come true, but mine..."

"My true Southern belle," Olivia began softly, holding onto her. "Your dream will come true too; you just have to be patient.

Annie leaned in kissing the sweet-smelling, quiet baby. She beamed a little smile at her tiny niece.

Now come inside; the Bellameads are back at Bella Oak," Olivia called out proudly.

Chapter Twenty-Nine
"Vincent Tolleson"

The news of the war grew with the Union winning many battles and the war continuing on. November the fifteenth, news came of General William Tecumseh Sherman's destroying Atlanta by burning much of the city. He led 60,000 soldiers to Savannah on his March to the Sea. The Union left everything in ruins in their 280 mile wake. Revenge for both sides had grown, and the fighting wasn't letting up with the casualties growing.

Joseph and Annie had their sixteenth birthdays. He was adamant about joining the troops, but Andrew held him back for a while, knowing the young boy didn't know the consequences of "War is hell."

Christmas celebration was small with Annie worried about Vincent and food becoming scarce. The new year of 1865 came in quietly at least for a few days. The tenth of January, Annie was sitting in the parlor knitting when she heard someone yelling and a wagon bouncing down the path to the house. Olivia handed Mary to Mama Bea and ran to the parlor. She grabbed Annie holding her back.

"We don't run out until we see who it is."

The girls saw Andrew and Joseph running from the barn so they hurried out the front door. There sitting on the seat of the wagon was Hansford Tolleson. He leaped from the wagon his clothes covered in blood.

"What's wrong?" Joseph screamed, dashing to the back of the wagon. He slid to a stop as his face drained, "Andrew, come here!"

The men picked up the young man lying in the back of the old wagon. Olivia gasped. Annie screamed and began to weave back and forth. Sadie helped her sit down on steps of the verandah. Olivia swung open the front door and the men laid the young man on the cot in the back room. Annie came running down the hallway, but Olivia grabbed her holding her back.

"Vincent," Annie called out softly.

Vincent, the young man Annie loved, lay there motionless on the cot. There were pieces of blood-soaked, torn-up sheets wrapped around his leg and arm

"Let Andrew work," Olivia whispered to Annie.

Andrew gently pulled off the dusty dressing on Vincent's leg. He sighed shaking his head. He began to clean the wound and work with precision. He then pulled the bandage off the young man's arm. Part of his arm and his left hand were missing. Annie gasped.

Andrew started tying tourniquets to slow the bleeding.

"Mama Bea," Andrew shouted, "Stoke up the fire in the kitchen stove, soak all the knife blades in vinegar and cold well water, then heat up all the blades in the fire."

"Yes sur," Mama Bea complied. "Joseph, yous' and Hansford goes and fetches me a bucket o' water from the well over yonder ter the side. That wells water wills be good and cold."

"Olivia, you and Annie go wait in the office. I'll send the boys there when they bring back the water," ordered Andrew.

The knives were submerged into the icy vinegar water for three minutes to kill germs. Then, Mama Bea placed the blades over the fire. When the blade tips started to change color, Mama Bea carefully using a tea towel handed the knives to Andrew.

Andrew used the red-hot blades to cauterize Vincent's wounds to stop the bleeding. He doused clean flour-sack towels into the well water and packed them over the wounds.

"Mama Bea, bring me some aloe vera and herbs from the pots in the kitchen," Andrew called out. He placed the gooey side of the leaves on the burns and put new sterile dressings over the leaves.

Andrew stood. "Thank you, Mama Bea. You are a fine medical assistant."

He walked into the office and Hansford met him. *How* was the only word that Andrew could muster.

"One of the other boys from the county was with Vincent during the battle. As soon as the field surgeon bandaged Vincent, the boy threw him over a horse that he stole and rode home. Dr. Holt isn't doing well and I remembered Joseph talking about you. We can't lose him, Andrew," he begged fidgeting with his hands.

"I'm going to do all I can." His eyes peered over to Olivia and Annie standing by the window. "Infection was already beginning in his leg and arm when you got him here. I cleaned out the wounds with cold water as best I could, but I will check the wounds daily and keep them as clean as possible."

Annie moved over by Andrew. "I want to see him."

"Annie, don't show remorse or sorrow; he doesn't need that. You have to be strong," Andrew said.

Olivia walked up next to her. "I'm not as strong as you," Annie whispered sobbing. "Olivia, he might lose his leg and he has already lost part of his arm and hand. It will devastate him."

"Not if it doesn't devastate you. First, he has to live, so no more tears, young lady," Olivia said.

Annie nodded her head and the sisters headed to the back room. Mama Bea had started to clean his good arm. Annie took his boots off and smiled. There hiding inside was a picture of her and the letters she had written. She looked back up at Olivia and smiled. She was going to fight this battle with Vincent and make her dream come true.

Olivia scooted the other cot next to Vincent, "Like father told me, we don't need you getting sick."

Annie sat down on the cot and laid a quilt over him. His face was pale. Lovingly, she touched his long dark hair.

Olivia went into the parlor and sat down. Joseph, Andrew, and Hansford were there. They were all quiet, just watching the logs burn in the fireplace.

"Hansford, that boy is in good hands now with Annie taking care of him," Olivia said, breaking the silence.

His eyes so like Vincent's looked over at her and then he smiled.

"Kobe said the fighting was horrible with blood and bodies everywhere. He heard that our generals are out maneuvered. The Union maybe winning! All the death and destruction may be for nothing," he finished shaking his head back and forth.

Andrew looked over at Hansford, and then bowed his head. Both men had seen the South reduced to rubble and mayhem, along with its men and boys. The once white cotton fields were bloody and strewn with bodies. Many of the magnificent plantations stood in ruins. Fatherless children, mothers, wives, sisters were left devastated. Only the old, the very young, Carpetbaggers and Scalawags were in attendance to rebuild.

Hansford left the next morning. He was afraid to leave his parents alone for fear of the Union soldiers coming this way. Annie sat vigilant by Vincent's bedside day and night, waiting and watching. Andrew meticulously cleaned and added new sterile dressings. Days went by with no improvement. Andrew was still worried about infection.

When Vincent finally opened his dark eyes, Annie shouted for Andrew. He came running squatting down beside Vincent.

"Son, how are you feeling? Are you in very much pain?"

"No, Sir," Vincent answered staring up at Andrew and Annie. "How did I get here?"

"Kobe brought you home and Hansford brought you here," Annie offered taking in a deep breath gripping her hands together anxiously.

"Then, you are Andrew?"

"Yes, that's right. I have heard much about you, Vincent," he said looking over at Annie.

"My hand, I don't feel my hand," he said trying to lift his arm.

"Son, you lost your left hand and part of your arm."

"No!" he shouted. "My leg hurts. Is it still there?"

"Yes, but the infection isn't good. I'm not going to lie to you. Mama Bea is boiling all the bandages and clothes we are using," he paused. "I clean your wounds every day, myself. We will see."

The young man turned his head from them and Annie's face drooped with worry. Andrew patted Vincent and leaned over whispering into Annie's ear. "Let him have some time."

Joseph stood by the door of the room seeing what the war had done to a strong, strapping, young man. He now was beginning to understand why Andrew and Olivia were against his participating in the military.

Annie wasn't giving up on Vincent making him sip chicken broth and talking to him of their future. He lay there hardly talking, staring up at the beautiful young girl he had hoped to marry.

One morning Annie couldn't stand his silence any longer. With tears building in her blue eyes, she left the room. Olivia saw her walk outside. Olivia looked out the window and saw that Annie's body was bent over and she was sobbing from exhaustion and trying to take on his pain.

She made her way to the back room. "Vincent, you know I don't hold back," Olivia began. The old cot creaked as she sat down. "I don't have any right to talk to you, but that never stopped me, as you well know."

His mouth curled up on the side with a frown, knowing she was so opposite of Annie.

"You, my friend, are acting like a jackass!" He flinched.

"That young girl loves you more than her life and you are turning her away."

"Olivia, I'm not a whole man, and she is so beautiful and perfect. She doesn't need me."

"Such foolish gibberish, you may think you are saving her from a life with a cripple, not a whole man, but you are breaking her caring heart. She sees you full of life, the boy who risked getting in trouble to spend time with her, teaching her to dance, not worrying about the consequences. A man who has plenty of life to give! Don't throw her life away along with yours." She stood back up. "I have seen too much death and waste. You are alive with all that has happened. Vincent, don't waste your life."

His dark eyes didn't blink, giving her an angry stare. How dare she talk to him that way!

Her dress swished as she made her way out of the room. She first stopped and looked out the window at her sweet sister. Annie's arms were wrapped around herself, standing out in the cold trying to get her composure back.

Olivia went to the office feeling the cool air by the window. She could see Andrew and Big John standing talking in the doorway of the barn as they watched Joseph out in the corral trying to break a new horse they had bought.

She quietly whispered, "Benjamin, I miss you so much."

She stepped slowly up the long staircase to the nursery to check on Mary. She stopped at the door listening as Mama Bea was rocking Mary singing softly. She turned back going to her bedroom not to disturb them. Mama Bea loved that baby and didn't care that she was a freed slave. This was her home and this was her baby to see to.

She heard a ruckus and quickly moved down the stairs.

Joseph was standing in the foyer with mud on him, grinning, "I did it, that horse was taught a few things,"

Andrew was standing behind him looking up at her.

"Joseph, get cleaned up. It's almost time for supper," she called out to the young man.

He grinned, the same grin that Benjamin used after one of his escapades. He ran past her up the stairs trying to touch her with muddy hands, giggling.

Supper was weak stew with a few canned vegetables from last summer and bread. Annie didn't make it to supper and she was worried.

Olivia went to the back room, but stopped before entering. It was quiet as she peered in and saw that Annie's head was on Vincent's chest, as he tenderly played with her hair. He smiled up at Olivia, and she nodded turning around softly closing the door. Her little Southern belle would, indeed, have her dreams coming true.

Chapter Thirty
"The War is Over"

The freshness of spring was in the air. The wild flowers were popping their heads out of the ground, and the unplowed land was carpeted with red and white clover.

The rumors of bloody battles in Richmond grew as well. Buildings were lit a fire as the Confederates retreated, leaving Richmond to the Union soldiers.

One day toward the end of May, a lone rider rode up to Bella Oak with a trail of dust behind him. Olivia, Annie, and Vincent were sitting on the verandah and could see that it was Hansford.

He started yelling before jumping off his horse, "General Robert E. Lee surrendered April ninth in Virginia. The war is over! The Confederacy is over! Our boys are all comin' home!"

Everyone stood still not able to say anything, knowing the cost the South had paid and would pay.

"The other news is…" Hansford continued, "April fifteenth, President Abraham Lincoln was shot and killed by a Southern sympathizer. Andrew Johnson is President now."

With the announcement of the war ending, Andrew stood not moving with tears in his eyes. Vincent's right hand held onto his left arm with the missing hand, knowing the price he had paid.

"Big John, Terrance, you are truly free now to live and do as you like," Olivia announced.

"I don't need no President to tell me what to do," Terrance said grabbing his son swinging him around in a circle as Benjamin squealed. "I want to stay right here on Bella Oak."

"Me toos, I can't leave Bella Oak," Big John added ducking his head down.

"Don't looks at me, I ain't leavin' my babies," Mama Bea assured hugging tightly to Mary turning back to the door, taking the child inside the house.

"Well, Olivia, I reckon I won't be going to war," Joseph proclaimed.

"Thank God. We are all safe," Olivia heaved a big sigh. "We will have to all work together side by side until Bella Oak can turn a profit. I have no money to pay anyone."

"Olivia," interrupted Andrew, "I have access to US currency through my father. I'll be able to pay people who work for us."

Vincent decided to go home with his brother, but not without asking Annie to marry him in November when she would turn seventeen. That would give him time to heal his physical wounds along with his emotional wounds.

The South would take decades to rebuild, but the people at Bella Oak were safe now. The natural order of some elements of life seemed to be taking shape, and that gave the inhabitants of Bella Oak hope.

Joseph and Annie had left with Big John to go see Ruth. She was considering coming home and Joseph had unfinished business with Madeline.

Chapter Thirty-One
"Carpetbaggers and scalawags"

With a grim face, Andrew stood in the office reading a letter from his father, John. He shook his head as he handed Olivia the letter. She quickly read the words and knew their meaning.

"Andrew, I understand," she whispered walking near him wrapping her arms around him. He took in a deep breath and she held onto him tighter. "You tell him someday Mary and I will visit, too. I do hope he is doing better soon."

He reluctantly planned a trip to care for his father, leaving his young wife and daughter alone. Olivia stood on the Verandah holding onto him firmly as he kissed her and Mary. It was still very dangerous for him to travel north. The war might officially be over, but many in the South didn't believe the end had come, and there was no denying his Northern accent.

Carpetbaggers and scalawags were taking advantage of the torn and destroyed South. The war was over, but the division wasn't.

She stood watching Andrew ride out of Bella Oak waving back to her and Mary. Again, she would be waiting to hear from him. Praying he would be safe and come home soon was all she could do.

Days, then weeks went by without any word. Each day she would sit and gently hold Mary rocking back and forth. In her mind, she could see Andrew holding his daughter. She was hanging on to hope.

"Olivia," Terrance called out waving a letter in his hand.

She sat down seeing it was a letter from Annie, not Andrew. They would be coming home soon from Charleston along with Ruth. Ruth had readily agreed to come home to plan a wedding for Annie and Vincent. A celebration at Bella Oak would boost everyone's spirits.

The old plantation's Southern belle was getting married! Ruth was already planning for everyone to be there, Lawrence and Mary Jane, Camille and Jerrold along with Jackson and Etta. Bella Oak would come alive again.

The last page of the letter was from Joseph. He had asked Madeline to marry him next year. He was so excited that he could pop! He couldn't wait to bring Madeline home to Bella Oak. The Bellamead name would continue on.

Life was quiet for the next few weeks as the scent of the pine needles parched in the heat of the sun. Olivia had worked in the garden early that morning. As she was about to go inside with a basket of vegetables, Terrance brought her a letter from Andrew. She was so excited to finally get word from him. She stuffed the letter in her apron pocket and headed to the kitchen with the vegetables.

Then, Olivia headed out front to sit on the verandah and read Andrew's letter. She saw a cloud of dust and four men riding directly for her with rifles in their hands. She panicked. She was not wearing the Catawba whistle and she did not have her pistol.

"Well now, look what we have here, a pretty thing," one mocked for all of them as they stepped up onto the verandah. She stood stoically trying not to panic. One man walked right up to her and ran his hand down her body. He smelled rotten, inside and out.

"Let's get to work," the short, round man with missing teeth shouted. "Then we can have some fun," he snarled looking over at Olivia.

The tall bearded man grabbed her arm and dragged her into the parlor. Olivia bit him. The man shoved her to another man.

"Let me go! Let me go, now!" Olivia demanded as she pulled away.

"Look, this plantation hasn't been touched. We have hit the jackpot," the first man declared.

He started picking up things around the room. She cringed as the man grabbed up anything of value knocking everything in his way to the floor demolishing the beautiful room.

"Go on out to the barn," the leader told the short, stocky man who followed his order.

One of the other men pushed Olivia into a chair by the window. Olivia leaned to the side of the chair. She gasped. She could see smoke coming from the huge barn.

The man rolled out a wagon up to the side door. Her heart was breaking, knowing the home would probably be next.

The other men began to fill the wagon with valuables. The leader watched Olivia with anticipation. The short, stocky man made sure the items in the wagon were arranged for traveling.

It didn't take long for the men to go on a rampage through the large home. She could hear glass-breaking, doors slamming. Her body trembled trying to come up with a plan.

She heard Mama Bea scream from upstairs in the nursery. Olivia panicked.

"Mary...," Olivia thought.

She was keeping track of the men: one upstairs, one inside the back rooms, one by the wagon, then there was the one keeping watch over her.

"You watchin' me? I see you lookin'. How long has it been since you had a real man in this house?" he laughed.

She tighten her fist as he approached her. He lifted her up from the chair pulling her close staring at her face with a nasty smile on his face.

"Soon, my lovely. That's a promise. Business first, then pleasure."

He yanked her arm pulling her into the dining room. She tried to get away, but he overpowered her and pushed her face-down on the table.

He held her stable and yelled to the other man in the back of the house, "Hank, you about done out there?"

But, no answer. He held her down with one hand by the back of her neck. Olivia started screaming and struggling.

"Go ahead, scream. The more you scream, the more I like it."

Then, a shot rang out and the man fell backward to the floor. Blood pumped out of his chest as he gurgled blood with his last breath.

She looked over at the door. "Terrance, there are three more of them," she whispered, quickly turning hurrying to go get her gun, but Terrance grabbed her.

"No, Olivia, we got all four."

"Mary," Olivia screamed, running up the stairs. There at the top of the stairs was Mama Bea holding tight to Mary with one of the men lying on the floor by the door of the nursery, stabbed to death with a big butcher knife.

Terrance knew Mama Bea wouldn't hesitate to defend herself or those she loved. He lifted the dead man over his shoulder carrying him down the stairs. He had to go outside to make sure the fire didn't spread beyond the barn.

"We'ze be alright. Dat mans shor' weren't going ter touch this sweet baby," she said turning back to the nursery.

Olivia hurried over to Mama Bea wrapping her arms around her.

"Thank you," Olivia cried out.

Mary wiggled in Mama Bea's arms as the old woman passed the baby to Olivia. Mama Bea sat down in the rocker and gently motioned for Olivia to give Mary to her. Mama Bea began singing and rocking as she worked her magic with Mary. The baby fell asleep all snuggled in the arms of safety, as if nothing had happened.

Chapter Thirty-Two
"Southern Dreams"

Olivia made her way down the towering staircase and out onto the verandah seeing Terrance out front.

"Everyone is safe?" she questioned.

"Yes, Sadie and Benjamin was with my mother. Them men, they didn't bother the slaves quarters. Are yo' alright? We weren't going to let those men hurt anyone, not now."

Olivia nodded her head yes pulling in a deep breath remembering the touch and smell of dirty, deplorable avarice.

"Terrance, when is this ever going to end?

"Olivia, I don't know," he ducked his head down. "When I was out in the field, a gust of wind hit me and I heard a voice that said, 'go home.' It was the voice of Benjamin," he explained, peering at her strangely.

"Yes, Benjamin is still protecting us. Thank you, Terrance; you saved our lives and Bella Oak."

She could see the sadness in his face. He was missing Benjamin as he stepped down the verandah. More bodies to bury!

Her hands tightened onto the pillar supporting the verandah. Staring out to the once beautiful fields, she closed her eyes remembering the white fluffy cotton blooming as far as her eyes could see with the soft clouds floating across the blue sky leaving shadows over the fields.

Music began to play in her head, the *Virginia Reel* medley. She could feel Andrew's arm caressing her and swirling her on the dance floor. A smile came on her face with the memories of seeing her young Yankee beau from her bedroom. She felt the same emotions of that day so long ago. Her heart began to beat faster. She could see neighbors and friends, some standing proud and others sitting on spreads covering Bella Oak's grounds. They sang *Dixie Land* with their voices reverberating over the hills.

She could hear Big John's voice so strong singing the new song of the South.

Oh, Polly! Oh, Polly! It's for your sake alone,
I left my dear old father, my country and my home,
I left my dear old mother to weep and to mourn,
I am a Rebel Soldier and far from my home.

Smelling the smoke from the barn, she choked, coughed, and cried by herself. So much death and so many lives ruined with the rape and destruction of the south. And, over what? She didn't think she would ever understand. Her tired eyes peered over at the ashes of the barn understanding that could easily have been Bella Oak. She sighed from fatigue and stress and awareness of exactly what had happened that day.

She looked out to the huge, old, twisted oak across from the spring fed creek that had withstood years of hardship but still surviving. She could see Andrew sitting up in the old tree so excited like a small boy climbing to the top.

"Father, I will bring Bella Oak back. I promise I won't let you or her down… Benjamin and I will help protect her," she called out. "We will have our Southern dreams and will live for generations to come."

A wisp of cool air touched her and there standing tall looking down on her was Benjamin. He was so handsome with his kind face; just as the day he left for Charleston to warn the Confederates.

"Benjamin," she whispered, "did I die…was this all a dream?"

"No, my sweet, Olivia, you are alive and well."

"Then how can I see you like Father did?"

"Because," his head lowered, "you needed me."

"My sweet brother, thank you for warning Terrance and keeping us safe."

He grinned, that mischievous grin, and disappeared into the air.

"Thank you, Benjamin," she softly whispered again holding onto the massive pillar wishing she could hold on to him longer.

She reached into her apron pocket with trembling fingers and pulled out the unopened letter.

"Oh, Andrew, please come home soon," she cried out.

Tears flowed down splashing onto the envelope she held next to her heart. She clinched it tight.

"How much more must my mind manage? How much more must I bear!"

Her eyes peered down staring at the handwriting, Andrew's precise handwriting.

About the Author

Diann Shaddox is a Native American Indian and a member of the Wyandotte Nation of Oklahoma and she has Essential Tremors. She's an award-winning author of *A Faded Cottage, Whispering Fog, Miranda, Spirits of Sacred Mountain, The Gatekeeper,* and *Southern Dreams* Series.

Diann is the Founder of Diann Shaddox Foundation, a Non-Profit 501c(3) public organization fighting the battle to find a cure and bring awareness for Essential Tremor, (ET).

Diann was born on December 18th in a small southern town of Nashville, Arkansas, the youngest and only daughter of William and Mary Ann Shaddox. But, fate stepped in and William, a crop-duster, at the age of 25, died in a plane crash on November 20th, a month before she was born, therefore, Diann was never able to meet her father. Mary Ann, who grew up in Miami, Oklahoma, moved back to Miami after William's death, where Diann lived until her mother died when she was only 3 years old. Diann then moved to Nashville, Arkansas to live with her grandparents. At the age of 10, Diann's Granddad died of a stroke, leaving her grandmother alone to see to her.

Diann learned from an early age about death and how life should not be squandered. Her Mamow, who had lost her right hand in an accident at a factory in Nashville, Arkansas, taught her, you never give up. Her grandmother never let anything stand in her way. She taught herself to write, cook, and even how to sew and make quilts with her left hand, without any prosthetics. Being handicapped was a word she never used.

Growing up in a small town was wonderful, learning to fish, growing a garden and the most important thing, patience of a grandmother. Stories from the past evolved of family bringing many stories to life. Sitting out late at night on cool summer evenings, swinging on an old swing staring up at the stars helped Diann's vivid imagination grow.

On May 20, 2014, Diann's son Rick died of a brain tumor.

She has an enthusiasm for travel and living life to its fullest. You have only one life and shouldn't waste it. The zest for meeting and getting to know people is a very important component in her life. She is a believer of herbs, natural and organic foods, and a big supporter of Bio-identical Hormones and keeping our planet green.

Diann has resided in eight great states, Arkansas, Oklahoma, Kentucky, New Jersey, Virginia, Texas, Florida, and now South Carolina.

www.diannshaddox.com

Diann Shaddox Foundation for Essential Tremor

The Diann Shaddox Foundation for Essential Tremor is a Non-Profit 501 c(3) public organization.

Diann Shaddox Foundation for Essential Tremor mission is to advance knowledge and recognition of Essential Tremor to the world and find treatments and a cure for Essential Tremor. We will change the future for everyone who will inherit or develop Essential Tremor by offering hope and assistance for people suffering from hardships magnified by Essential Tremor.

We want to show that Essential Tremor isn't just for the elderly, but children of all ages have ET. Most people though haven't heard about Essential Tremor and Diann Shaddox Foundation for Essential Tremor is adamant to bring attention to the world.

Essential Tremor (ET) is a progressive neurological condition that causes a rhythmic trembling of the hands, head, voice, legs, or body. ET can begin at any age, from birth to 100 and doesn't discriminate with age, race, sex, or national origin. Over 100 million people worldwide have Essential Tremor.

To learn more, go to www.diannshaddoxfoundation.org

HISTORY OF CROSSWAYS, AIKEN, SC
THE PLANTATION HOME ON ALL
SOUTHERN DREAMS BOOK COVER

Distinctly Southern and an integral part of Aiken's history, Crossways was built before the incorporation of Aiken, before the Hitchcock's and the Winter Colony put Aiken on the map, and before John Gary Evans belted out his acceptance speech for the nomination to the office of governor from the second story balcony.

Circa 1815, Crossways was built by the burgeoning cotton industry that flourished before the Civil War. The home was the centerpiece of a 368 acre cotton plantation in what was then the Barnwell District. Though little is known about the property prior to the Civil War, in 1868 it was purchased by James L Derby, a New York publisher and partner in the Aiken Land Improvement Company. Derby moved his family to Aiken in 1868. The property at that point had been sold down to 25 acres and was often referred to as Derby Farm or Derby Mansion.

The Derby Mansion with 25 acres was sold to Henry Watkins in 1872. The Watkins owned the property until 1875, when they sold the home and 25 acres to Edward Henry.

Henry was from Boston, but he was a Southern sympathizer and had settled for a time in Charleston. Here he met his future wife, Harriet Lythgoe, and became a shipbuilder and blockade runner.

For several years the home was occupied, but not owned by John Gary Evans. Evans served in the SC House and Senate and was elected Governor in 1894.

In 1899 the home and 30 acres was acquired from the estate of Mrs. Henry by a prominent Aiken dentist, H.G. Ray for $5,500. The family of George Monroe was known to have lived in the home in the early 1900's. It seems the name "Crossways" came into being about this time.

It has been suggested to stem from the irregular, crossways setting of the home on the property.

Ray sold the property in 1927 for $40,000 to Arthur Young, an accountant and business man. Arthur Young founded Arthur Young & Company, an international accounting firm which ultimately has become part of the Ernest & Young firm. Young spent another $35,000 doing major additions and changes to the home as reported in local news of 1927. Young died in 1948 after which the property was sold to P.J. Boatwright, a cotton merchant.

The Boatwright's desired to have their four children nearby and deeded lots facing Banks Mill Road to each; shrinking the property to 2 acres as the housing boom demanded land for families coming to Aiken. In 1954, Mr. & Mrs. Harold Sanders from Dallas, Texas came to Aiken with the Savannah River Plant and acquired the home.

In 1987 the home was sold to Canadians, William & Leslie Stirling as a winter residence. Mr. Stirling took the task of documenting the house's history and significance and got it placed on the National Registry of Historic Places in 1996.

In 1998 Wisconsin transplants, Patrick & Gail Pratt purchased the property.

In 2007, Bob & Jane Hottensen, also from Wisconsin purchased the property as a winter retreat.

With continued respect to Crossways, the Hottensen's undertook the most ambitious recent renovations, including annexation of several residential lots around Crossways. Their efforts have integrated the home into a much larger presentation – fitting of its name – Crossways Plantation.

Over 200 years old now, Crossways represents the grace, ease, and elegance of a time past.